Praise for Hideo Yokoyama:

'He's a master' *New York Times*

'Addictive' *The Times*

'Very different . . . to almost anything out there'
Observer

'Yokoyama possesses that elusive trait of the first-rate
novelist: the ability to grab readers' interest and never let go'
Washington Post

'An education about Japan'
David Peace

ᴐrn in 1957, Hideo Yokoyama worked for twelve years as an
ᴉnvestigative reporter with a regional newspaper north of Tokyo,
ᴣfore becoming one of Japan's most acclaimed fiction writers.
efecture D is his third work to be translated into the English
ᴉguage.

Jonathan Lloyd-Davies studied Japanese at Durham and Chinese
at Oxford. His other translations include *Edge* by Koji Suzuki,
which received the Shirley Jackson award for best novel.
Originally from Wales, he now resides in Tokyo.

Also by Hideo Yokoyama

Six Four
Seventeen

HIDEO YOKOYAMA

PREFECTURE D

Translated from the Japanese by Jonathan Lloyd-Davies

riverrun

First published in the Japanese language as *Kage no kisetsu* (Season of Shadows) by Bungeishunju Ltd in Tokyo in 1998

First published in Great Britain in 2019 by riverrun
This paperback edition published in 2019 by

riverrun
An imprint of
Quercus Editions Ltd
Carmelite House
50 Victoria Embankment
London EC4Y 0DZ

An Hachette UK company

A CIP catalogue record for this book is available
from the British Library

· ISBN 978 1 78648 466 6 (PB)
ISBN 978 1 78648 465 9 (EBOOK)

10 9 8 7 6 5 4 3 2 1

Typeset by CC Book Production

Printed and bound in Great Britain by Clays Ltd, Elcograf S.p.A.

Papers used by Quercus are from well-managed forests and other responsible sources.

CONTENTS

SEASON OF SHADOWS

I

The room was shut away from the wind and the myriad sounds of spring. The windows were permanently closed, concealed behind heavy, tightly drawn curtains. The air conditioning seemed to be on, but a brief session at a desk was enough to realise that it barely worked, despite the racket.

The Administration annexe was a little over sixteen square metres, located on the first floor of the north building of the Prefecture D Police Headquarters. To mark the fact that it was not in common use, it was often referred to as 'the spring house' or 'the retreat'. These terms were, of course, only used by the staff of Administration. The rest of the force chose to feign disinterest and call it simply 'Personnel', some with a knowing grin, others with a hint of trepidation in their eyes.

They'll be up there now, barricaded in Personnel.

That was what they all said.

With internal notification due in five days, the work on compiling the annual list of transfers was in its final stages. With no more than 3,000 career and non-career officers under review, and an even smaller number of these actually up for transfer, the pieces of the puzzle would, in any normal year, have already fallen into place.

But there had been a delay, following an inauspicious call from

Internal Affairs that afternoon. The captain of Station S in the north had, it seemed, pressured a landscaper from a resort in his jurisdiction to construct a garden at his wife's family home, for a fee that essentially amounted to nothing.

Bloody fool.

Shinji Futawatari cursed at the image of the man now pictured on his monitor.

The captain, whose oval features suggested a gentle nature, had only assumed the post the previous spring. As such, he had not been included in the list of candidates up for transfer. The knowledge of his transgression, however, meant it would no longer do to leave him visible to the public as the station's representative. The director of Administrative Affairs had left Futawatari with specific instructions to redraft the plans by the following morning, to make sure they included the captain's reassignment.

Futawatari had a long history with Personnel. For a total of six years as assistant inspector and inspector, then two more following his promotion to superintendent and subsequent assignment to overseeing the broader management of the force as Administration inspector, he had always been involved in the process of drafting transfers. It was unlikely the executive would consider letting someone of his experience move on. Not, at least, until the section – which scraped by on a minimal headcount – was upgraded to a division.

He was no stranger to situations like this.

He'd worked under a captain who had been particularly susceptible to flattery. Like a foolish prince, the man had ordered one incredible promotion after another. He'd seen a succession of Administrative Affairs directors, each of whom had sought to flex their authority in order to interfere with the pieces of the puzzle, paying no heed to local realities or conventions. There

4

was, he realised, no point in getting worked up whenever something like this cropped up. The often arbitrary requirements of these self-centred bureaucrats meant it was all but tradition for the process to require a series of all-nighters.

Still, this was the first time he'd been forced to consider a change just when he'd been preparing to send the list across to Welfare and Officer Development for printing, having already obtained the captain's stamp of approval. There was also the fact that it was not simply due to the whim of some career bureaucrat but rather the reprehensible actions of a *captain*, someone who was supposed to be on the same side.

It was enough to stoke even Futawatari's anger.

Have him sleep it off somewhere, maybe Licensing or Training.

Futawatari dragged his mouse across the organisational chart on the screen, searching for a suitable destination.

Whenever a front-line member of the executive did something to cause a loss of face, it was usual to reel them in to some out-of-sight post in headquarters, to box them up and let them cool off for four or five years. You had to avoid transfers that were an obvious step down – that would risk catching the attention of the press – and Futawatari realised that some of the veteran reporters knew the inner workings of the force better than many of the officers themselves. That brought the danger that the transgressions would be made public. Fortunately, it was a particular strength of Personnel to nurture posts that were both impenetrable and obscure, enabling transfers that were recognisable from the inside as punitive yet justifiable to the outside as existing to 'strengthen department X or Y'.

What would be the best move?

Assuming, then, that the captain was bound for Licensing or Training, the next step would be to transfer a suitable

management-level officer to the newly vacant position in Station
S. A straight swap would be preferable, but it would be too big
a step up for the current chief of Licensing to assume a captain's
post. Even more of a problem was the chief of Training. His age
and experience were good, but his hometown was in the station's
jurisdiction. Such a move was taboo and would bring questions.
Futawatari would have no choice but to offer special justification
for the transfer.

Asshole.

Futawatari cursed again. He took a deep breath, then set about
tearing apart the pieces of the already approved puzzle. He would,
after all, have to do this one step at a time. Move the chief of
Licensing to Station G, one grade below Station S. Return the
captain of Station G to Juvenile Crime in the Prefectural HQ.
Take the chief of Juvenile Crime and slide him over to Community Safety. Move the chief of Community Safety to . . .

'Futawatari. A minute, if you don't mind.'

He looked up, still scowling, to see Administration Chief
Shirota beckoning from behind the half-open door of the main
entrance. There were no phones in the annexe. This was mostly
for show, the idea being to stop information leaking out while
simultaneously preventing anyone from calling in for special
treatment. Shirota was the highest-ranking division chief in the
Prefectural HQ, yet even he had to make his way down multiple
corridors to get here from Administrative Affairs, which was
located on the first floor of the main building, and take the long
walk over the tiled passageway that connected the two buildings.
Futawatari nodded and got to his feet. For the first time in hours,
he glanced at the clock on the wall.

It was a little after nine in the evening.

'Something's come up. If you'd be kind enough to accompany

me to the director's office?' That Shirota was frowning was obvious even in the dim light of the corridor.

Trouble?

'Sir, if this is related to the captain, I've already started—' Futawatari stopped partway through the ill-considered sentence. Shirota had already been apprised of the issue of the captain, meaning something else would have brought him all this way. And he'd intimated that the director of Administrative Affairs was still in his office, at a time when he would usually be at home, tipping back a glass of brandy. Futawatari hurried back to his desk. He closed the windows still open on his screen and took out the disk and he locked it in the safe. He hurried out to follow Shirota's nervous-looking figure down the corridor.

Futawatari looked pale, even away from the computer.

Something more urgent than this?

They made their way towards the main building, walking along corridor after corridor until they reached the red carpet which stretched all the way to the captain's office in the distance. There was a glow, ahead and to the right, coming from the window of the director's office. Straightening his posture, Futawatari followed Shirota in. The tread of the carpet was immediately thicker. Director Oguro, who was sitting on a couch, turned his head to greet them. His eyes were narrow and displeased.

'Something's come up.' Oguro motioned a hand at a second couch, not waiting for them to sit as he growled the same words as Shirota.

'Trouble, sir?'

Shirota's eyes rose, hesitant to meet Futawatari's gaze. Futawatari, for his part, was already braced for bad news.

'It's Osakabe. He has informed us that he doesn't intend to step down.'

'What?' Futawatari blurted, failing to mask his surprise.

'It seems he intends to make trouble,' Oguro said, not even trying to hide his irritation as he fixed a glare on Futawatari's stunned eyes.

But that's . . . unthinkable.

Michio Osakabe. One of the force's more prominent alumni, the man had been director of Criminal Investigations when he'd taken voluntary retirement three years ago, settling thereafter into an executive position created by Administrative Affairs. His tenure had been set to expire before the upcoming batch of transfers. His successor had been pegged as Director Kudo in Community Safety, now scheduled for retirement himself.

The puzzle will fall apart.

Shirota had called Osakabe at home, just an hour earlier, to discuss the details of the handover. When he'd broached the topic, however, Osakabe had told him he wouldn't be leaving and unilaterally ended the call.

Futawatari's heart was racing. *Osakabe refusing to step down.* That would leave Kudo with nowhere to go. One of the key roles of Administration was to develop positions for executives to take upon retirement from the force. It was a chance for the division to prove its worth. Personnel would become a laughing stock should they fail to procure a post for someone as high-ranking as the director of Community Safety, leaving him without a position for a year. And any failure of Personnel would reflect badly on the division as a whole.

Damn it.

'Did he say why?' Futawatari asked. He'd tried to sound composed but his voice had come across as strained.

'If he had, this would be easy,' Oguro snapped.

Oguro both despised and feared failure at any level. Born in the southern reaches of the prefecture, he'd made police sergeant at his local headquarters and spent time manning a nearby substation. Some years later, perhaps due to some personal epiphany, he'd decided to take – and subsequently passed – the promotion exams, securing himself a future as a career officer. Yet he remained in many ways a kind of hybrid. While he could throw his weight around in the prefectures, he was still small fry as far as Tokyo was concerned. Sectioned off from the purebred bureaucrats and their race to the top, he had been transferred from region to region, occasionally landing himself an unexceptional role in Tokyo but suffering the whole time the particular anguish that came with having no faction of his own. At his age, he had maybe one or two postings left. He would hope to secure a captain's post before he had to hang up his uniform. A small station would do – maybe somewhere in the plains, where the climate was good.

Don't you fucking mess this up for me.

To Futawatari, the threat was almost audible.

'Section Chief Uehara can take over the work on the transfers. I want you to find out what's behind Osakabe's change of heart.'

It was clear that Shirota had heard the warning, too; his eyes had been pleading as he instructed Futawatari to investigate.

2

As he made his way back along the dark corridor, Futawatari felt like burying his head in his hands. While Shirota hadn't exactly said as much, it was evident that he wanted Futawatari to fix the situation. Osakabe's plans aside, those of the force were already in motion. Futawatari would have no choice but to hand the man his notice. That much was unavoidable. *Isn't this your job?* Futawatari had suppressed the urge to comment. He'd already known how Shirota, always quick to protect his own interests, would have responded: *You, more than anyone, know the background to this post.*

Six months prior to Osakabe's scheduled retirement a group of construction companies had approached Administration with a proposal to establish a foundation to monitor industrial dumping. It hadn't been chance that the timing had coincided with a spate of corruption charges being made against the industry. Having wracked their brains as to how to improve relations with the Prefectural HQ, the companies had come up with the idea of establishing a foundation and offered up the post of executive.

Administration had, for its part, welcomed the idea. They were always in need of good executive-level positions and that year had in fact been struggling to place a number of senior officials who were due for retirement but had nothing in the pipeline. While the division did not expect to grant any special favours should the industry suffer an investigation, its discomfort at having consciously ingested poison was real, obscured only by the fact that the subject was never openly discussed.

The director of Administrative Affairs had appointed Osakabe as the first managing director of the foundation on the condition that his term would be a maximum of three years. In Prefecture D, the usual tenure for this kind of post ranged between three and six years. Osakabe's term had been set at the shortest end of the scale in order to balance the number of executives due for retirement in the next five years against the number of positions that were expected to become available.

Had Osakabe been unhappy with this? It was the first thought to come to mind. Back when the post had been announced, Futawatari had been a section chief in Personnel. He'd run the numbers himself. He'd handed in the conclusion.

Or . . .

A second, more disconcerting scenario crept into view. A private office; a secretary; a car and chauffeur; a salary at least as good as his old one. What if it had all become too comfortable to give up? It wasn't, Futawatari supposed, entirely unthinkable. If Osakabe *had* become greedy, that would complicate the matter. While his term was fixed at three years, the contract was only verbal. As with any gentleman's agreement, it was effective only until one side announced their intention to tear it up.

This had, of course, never happened.

The force, more than any other organisation, existed within its own, closed community. You issued your first cries the moment you entered police school. You committed your life to the organisation and you remained a part of it until the day you died. Retirement meant nothing more than the end of your time on active duty. It had no bearing on your status as a member of the force. In this context, the gentleman's agreement came to symbolise more than just a promise. It became law. For Osakabe to ignore this and turn his back on the force – the idea seemed absurd. It would be akin to suicide, marking the end of his life with the police.

Having returned to Personnel, Futawatari informed Uehara that he was to take over the rebuilding of the puzzle. He issued a few brief pointers then sat at his own desk. He slid a disk marked 'Alumni' into the computer drive, took a deep breath then brought Michio Osakabe's file up on the screen.

The man's record remained impressive.

He had joined the force when it had still been under local governance. He'd worked at a substation as a police sergeant and made a succession of arrests for bike theft. From there, he'd received a transfer to Criminal Investigations in district. After three more years specialising in cases of theft, he'd been called to join Violent Crime as part of Criminal Investigations, First Division, in the Prefectural HQ. The section, with its focus on violent crime and murder, was one of the most prestigious in the force. Osakabe continued to move from post to post in district, but he never once strayed from his focus on violent crime. He spent a total of fourteen years like this, five of them as team leader. From there he charted a swift course up the ranks, making assistant chief in First Division, then chief advisor, then division chief. Finally, he made director, claiming for himself the number-one role in Criminal Investigations.

During the same period, he had also been chief of Criminal Investigations in district, served as captain of two stations and worked as sub-leader and then leader for Mobile Investigations. His secondment record, too, was beyond reproach; he had taken a two-year stint at Investigative Planning at the National Police Agency in Tokyo.

He had left only two significant cases unsolved. The first was an armed bank robbery, the investigation of which he'd led during his time as chief of First Division. The second was the savage murder of a female office worker, which had taken place soon after his promotion to director. It seemed, in comparison, impossible to tally up the number of cases he'd personally brought to a close. Futawatari used his mouse to scroll through the list, but it seemed to go on for ever.

He let out a deep sigh.

There was the usual sense of admiration. Osakabe's career in the force encompassed forty-two years, and not once had he ever thought to leave Criminal Investigations. There were other detectives working the front lines who maybe came close in terms of duration. Yet Futawatari knew, with utter certainty, that none would rise to the position of director, despite having devoted their lives to the department.

The regions were not structured like the central hubs, such as the Metropolitan Police Department. Everything here, from an organisational perspective, was concentrated in one of five major departments: Administrative Affairs, Security, Criminal Investigations, Community Safety and Transport. The directors of Administrative Affairs and Security were sourced from the NPA in Tokyo, which left only three director-level positions available for regional officers to aspire to. Of these, Criminal Investigations was the most prestigious.

It would seem natural, of course, for a detective who had spent his whole career in the department to assume the post of commander-in-chief, but the truth was that it hardly ever panned out this way. Detectives who ran cases twenty-four seven were left with little time to study for exams and, even when they somehow managed to prepare for them, there were still stories of old-guard detectives getting their candidates drunk the night before their exams. It was, instead, the officers who devoted some of their time to detective work, while spending the majority of it else-where – where they could chalk up results *and* manage to progress through the exams – who eventually secured the promotion.

It even happened, depending on the given situation, that the role was offered to officers who had never been posted to Criminal Investigations, officers who lacked even a rudimentary understanding of how to run an investigation. Priority for pro-motion to this, the most prestigious role in the regions, was in such cases usually given to whoever had made superintendent first in their particular generation.

And that meant Futawatari.

Having made superintendent at forty, he stood a head above his peers. He was thin, resembling a banker more than an officer of the law, unsure even of how to make an arrest, yet his long experience in Personnel had taught him that he would, in ten to fifteen years, be put forward as prime candidate for the role.

Whether he wanted it or not.

Perhaps this was why the details of Osakabe's career seemed mocking, overwhelming and why they brought about a sense of envy.

Don't think about it.

To end your career as director of Criminal Investigations, a post which symbolised the apogee of life as a detective – it was a dream that most officers entertained at least once in their lives.

Osakabe's case was, in many ways, unique in the history of Personnel. His, granted, had been a time when advancement had still been awarded not only to those who passed exams but also to those who demonstrated outstanding results in the field. And yet Futawatari couldn't help but suspect that luck had also played its part in the development of the man's career.

The man's features hovered at the top of the screen; dark, angular, glowering, with eyes like hollows, they were those of a detective. He was exactly the kind of man Futawatari had trouble understanding. The conclusion was groundless, of course, made back when Osakabe was still on active duty. The truth was that Futawatari had had little real contact with the man, despite having been part of the same organisation for over twenty years. He could still count on one hand the number of times they had met, either when he visited the man's office to discuss personnel or when summoned to listen to a budgetary request. Osakabe's habitat was the fourth floor and the various divisions of Criminal Investigations, while Futawatari's was the first and the collection of administrative functions contained within.

Futawatari realised he knew only the glowering expression he now saw in the man's photograph. He could not recall ever seeing the director laugh or lose his temper.

There's no choice. I'm going to have to confront him.

Futawatari tried to encourage himself as he noted down Osakabe's home address.

Bought the property. Mortgage repaid. Wife and three daughters. Eldest two married some time ago. Youngest currently living in Tokyo.

Futawatari gave Uehara, whose forehead was now glistening with sweat, a few more pointers, then left the building. Registering the cold wind, he popped up the collar of his coat.

It was already after midnight.

It didn't make sense. Why was Osakabe refusing to step down? Had three years been too short? Had he grown too comfortable to give up the benefits? Neither theory seemed to fit. The image from Osakabe's file, seen only moments earlier, was still vivid in his memory. Did he really mean it? That he would surrender his pride and disavow the force? Sell himself to industry and wade in their corruption?

For Director Osakabe to do this . . .

'Ridiculous,' Futawatari muttered, turning away from the main building, which was now in almost complete darkness.

There were only five days remaining until internal notification of the executive transfers. *Whatever this is about, I'll see him first thing tomorrow.* Futawatari picked up speed as he walked towards the parking area, feeling an apprehension quite different to that he'd experienced going into Director Oguro's office.

3

Futawatari missed Osakabe the next morning.

He'd been ready in his car at six, in the residential area where Osakabe lived. It hadn't taken long to find the plaque bearing the family name. Ringed by hedges of photinia, the two-storey building was strikingly modest for a man who had occupied the post of director. The neighbourhood was old, with roads that were traditional and narrow. Supposing it improper to park directly outside the man's home, Futawatari had retraced his steps and stopped on a patch of open land next to the river. *It's just a few minutes on foot. Walk around the house, keep an eye out, then call when it looks like they've finished breakfast.* Futawatari had formulated his plan and stepped out of the car.

Just as he'd set off, a black sedan had driven past, coming down the road that led from the city. Futawatari had seen a man with speckled grey hair in the driving seat. He hadn't been wearing a tie, but he'd been in a formal jacket, had firm shoulders and was wearing a pair of pristine white gloves. It had been too late when the understanding finally dawned. The sedan had turned into the residential area.

Futawatari was pale from running by the time the photinia had come into view in the distance. The white gloves were already closing the back door of the car. Shoulders heaving and unable to shout, Futawatari had simply watched, stunned, as Osakabe's profile, seen in the rear window, had glided by.

Back at his desk in Administration, Futawatari winced as he recalled the morning's failure. It was after seven thirty and his colleagues had begun to trickle in. He was usually the first in the office, so no one seemed surprised to see him. They would perhaps assume he had spent the night in the retreat, either working on the puzzle or on some other pressing task. He picked up the phone and pushed redial; he was beginning to get impatient. This was his fourth attempt. The phone continued to ring, telling him there was still no one at the foundation.

Where are you?

Osakabe had been picked up early that morning. Despite this, he had yet to arrive at the foundation. It was, Futawatari supposed, possible that he'd had an early appointment, maybe something out towards the mountains.

He got to his feet and pushed redial one more time. He was about to give up when Saito, one of the female officers posted to the section, came in with coffee. He thanked her and told her to leave it on his desk, that he'd drink it later, then left the office. Oguro and Shirota would be in soon. He couldn't report the morning's debacle and sensed it would be a good idea not to subject himself to the barrage of questions they would no doubt ask.

He checked in at the retreat. As expected, Uehara was there, wooden as he glared at his monitor with bloodshot eyes. He was balding but it was clear from the hair he did have that he hadn't been home to shower.

Futawatari took some time to help with the puzzle, even as he considered the idea of paying the foundation an unannounced visit.

If Osakabe were truly serious about holding on to his position, he would be keen to avoid any would-be assassins from Administration, especially during this sensitive period. Another day had passed, meaning only four remained until notification of the transfers. If Futawatari called ahead, if he failed to take the necessary precautions, there was a chance that Osakabe would go into hiding. If that happened, the fight would be over before it had even started. Still, Futawatari did not really expect a man like Osakabe to run. And if he was out when Futawatari arrived, someone at the foundation could always follow up for him. It was a little before noon when, having run the various scenarios through his mind, Futawatari took his leave of Uehara, whose eyes were still pleading.

It was five minutes on foot to Building F. The modern quasi-governmental building stood above the rest of the townscape, the blue-tinted panes of glass handsome as they reflected the steady flow of clouds. Inside, a high-speed lift whisked Futawatari to the eleventh floor. From there, following the sign, he walked down the corridor and found the foundation's nameplate a few doors on. The office was larger than he'd expected. There were ten or so desks, spaced generously apart, with dense green foliage cleverly placed to fill the gaps between them. Move one, even slightly, and the whole place would have looked more like an office in the middle of being set up.

A large topographic map was fixed to the wall on the right. The vast blueprint of the prefecture was dotted with a huge number of multicoloured pins. Red lines stretched from these, coming together in a radial pattern that traced the prefecture's many roads. Futawatari felt as though he were admiring a work of art.

He took a couple of steps forward and poked his head around a partition sectioning off an area next to the windows. With a view that stretched to the mountains bordering the prefecture in the distance, it was probably safe to assume that this was the office of the managing director. There was no one behind the partition's frosted glass.

As expected.

A young woman wearing a suit, model-like in her good looks, greeted him with flawless manners. Behind her came a nondescript older man who had appeared from somewhere behind one of the potted plants. After a brief exchange of business cards the man who had introduced himself as Director General Miyagi gave Futawatari a sceptical once-over. No doubt his image of the police was conditioned by Osakabe, his closest point of reference.

'I'm very sorry, but the managing director is out on business,' he said, not sounding in the least bit apologetic. He gestured towards a couch at the back of the room, his expression suggesting he could perhaps be of use instead.

Although this was the first time Futawatari had met Miyagi in person, he knew the man's background. He had, Futawatari recalled, spent a long period in the Prefectural Government as a section chief in Environmental Sanitation. The construction industry had offered the post of managing director to the police, and it appeared that they had not neglected those working in government. Whether that was true or not, Futawatari felt sure Miyagi's position was also one that had been arranged, and that, as such, he would be closely monitoring developments around Osakabe's refusal to step down. He might even have a sense of the reason behind it.

'Do you know where he is?'

'I think . . .' Miyagi mumbled, casting his attention to the map on the wall. 'Yes, he's on a site inspection in the north, although I couldn't tell you exactly where. The director, as I'm sure you know, is a very energetic man.'

'A site inspection?'

'That's when we investigate areas where we've had cases of illegal dumping.'

Of course. The pins in the map were there to mark dumping sites. The sheer quantity was astounding; hundreds at a glance. Futawatari had heard stories of lorries turning up with waste from the cities, but it was hard to fathom an operation on this scale.

Why was Osakabe conducting the inspections himself?

Futawatari considered the foundation's mission statement, which he'd read three years earlier. Their first responsibility was to educate, providing the private sector with guidelines on how to avoid unethical disposal companies while also distributing pamphlets appealing to the general populace to report cases of dumping. They were also responsible for on-site inspections when such reports came in. In certain cases, when their survey revealed unusually high levels of waste, or found it to be in the region of a water source, the foundation would compile their findings and request an official police investigation.

Osakabe's passion for the inspections was clear from Miyagi's tone. And yet a quick glance around the office was all it took to see that the foundation did not lack younger men, and men who seemed to have plenty of time on their hands. Even supposing they did lack the requisite manpower, it would still be odd for their managing director, who was sixty-three this year, to be dragging himself out in person.

'Does the director usually conduct the inspections himself?'

'Ah, well.' Miyagi looked vaguely uncomfortable. 'Yes, almost every day.'

'Almost every day?'

'For a year now, or thereabouts. I have suggested he get

someone else to do it, of course, but he insists on doing the legwork in person.'

Futawatari gave a nod to suggest he empathised before proceeding with his next question. 'Do you know when he'll be back?'

'Probably around five or six. It's possible he might go home directly, depending on how long the inspection takes.'

'Does he usually call in?'

'Not usually. We haven't heard from him today.'

Futawatari had been wrong to expect anything from Miyagi. It was hard to imagine this man, who was chained to the office and at Osakabe's beck and call, having any insight into the director's thoughts.

The chances of getting anything useful from him were slim.

Futawatari gave a quiet sigh and returned his gaze to the map on the wall. Osakabe was out there somewhere. Futawatari couldn't guess the scale, but the map itself was enormous, possibly three metres square, with details of all the trunk roads, as well as the smaller roads that linked the prefecture's various cities, towns and villages; even the forest roads were included.

When he'd first entered the room the red pencil lines had seemed to take a radial pattern but, on closer examination, it was evident that they all originated from the foundation. They were a record of Osakabe's movements, branching out in all directions, charting an incredible number of routes, each ending in a pin that marked a dumping site. Many stretched deep into the mountains, suggesting that the transgressors had a preference for out-of-the-way locations. The majority of these followed trunk roads until they were clear of cities and within range of the mountains. Once there, they forked, splitting over and over, spreading like capillaries until they reached the various dumping sites.

The stepladder adjacent to the wall seemed to highlight the effort that would have been spent to record such a vast number of trails. The map looked to Futawatari like a testament to the foundation's – or Osakabe's – hard work.

The delivery of lunch gave Futawatari the excuse he needed to get to his feet.

I guess it's worth a try.

He started for the door, listening for the footsteps to confirm that Miyagi was following from behind. Keeping it casual, he turned around and lowered his voice. 'I assume you've heard the news?'

Miyagi appeared to know exactly what he was referring to. 'Ah yes, of course. It's been decided that the director's term will be extended.'

Futawatari had to work to keep his emotions in check as the lift swept him back to ground level. His feet were heavy as he walked back to the Prefectural HQ. Miyagi had appeared unshaken by the news and showed no sign of holding a grudge about it. He'd also seemed unaware of the trouble Osakabe was causing, having no doubt already congratulated the man after hearing he was staying on. Futawatari was becoming increasingly riled. Osakabe had made a unilateral decision to stay on. In his mind, there was no conflict. He was simply deciding his own path, as though the police force didn't even exist. Did it stem from arrogance? Or from the man's confidence in his ability to get the job done?

Whatever the case, Futawatari realised he still had no grasp on the crux of the issue: *the motivation behind Osakabe's decision*. A young, female secretary. A spacious, comfortable office. A car and chauffeur at his disposal from the break of dawn. It was cosy. Of course it was cosy.

But there was something else to consider.

Force of habit.

Hurrying to the scene after a civilian tip-off. Combing through the detritus, finding a clue that might lead to the source. It was all too similar to the work of a detective. Fixing a map to a wall, adding pin after pin to mark the sites of investigation. The picture was an exact match to that of an Investigative HQ tracking down its quarry.

Once a detective . . .

He couldn't help thinking it. Futawatari saw again the topographical map, only now it was overlaid with the dazzling career he'd reviewed the previous evening. Was the man having some kind of breakdown? The idea sent a chill down his spine.

I don't know anything for sure. Not yet.

Shirota threw him a look when he walked back into Administration. Futawatari guessed it meant the director wanted to see them. He was getting ready when he saw the coffee, still there on his desk. A thin gathering of dust sat on its surface. *Leave it on my desk, I'll drink it later.* He felt his tension subside. He narrowed his eyes and saw Officer Saito, sitting perfectly straight, her back facing him. He couldn't comment on her qualities as a woman but he suspected she would do well for herself in the force.

He took a sip of the drink, hot five hours ago, then hurried out after Shirota. With nothing to report, he steeled himself in preparation for the director's mood, which no doubt would be bitter, like the coffee.

4

Futawatari paid Osakabe another visit at home that evening, but the director was still out.

With his wife away, too, the house was silent. Futawatari found a nearby park with some swings and a slide and decided to wait. There were no kids and no young mothers to call out to them. Everything around him felt aged.

Oguro's threat was no longer just implied. He'd slammed his fist on his desk when he'd heard of Futawatari's failure to get in touch with Osakabe. There had been a stack of newly printed business cards on the surface, Kudo's name printed next to the title Managing Director. Shirota had been to the printers and intercepted them before they were sent to Community Safety.

Kudo had not, it seemed, been informed of the problem.

Listen to me. I don't care how you do it. You track him down, today, and you order *him to step down.*

Futawatari glanced at his watch. It was after five thirty, the time he'd told himself he would try the house again. He jumped to his feet and started to walk. It was growing dark but there were still no lights on in the two-storey building.

Futawatari had already confirmed that Osakabe was not at the foundation, calling several times as he paced around the park. They'd gained him nothing more than Miyagi's repeated apologies.

I suppose I could try again.

He started to walk away from the house.

'May I help with something?'

He turned to see a dignified-looking woman in her sixties coming around the corner with some grocery bags in her hands. He recognised the modesty in her expression. Many of the police officers had wives who promoted themselves in line with their husband's advancement. The continued humility of Osakabe's wife was, in this context, the subject of much praise. Futawatari had met her once, at a party to celebrate Osakabe's career following his retirement from the force. She appeared to remember him.

'You're with Administrative Affairs, aren't you?' she asked, unassuming as she looked him in the eye. 'Come and wait inside. I'm sure my husband will be back soon.'

'Thank you, but it's not urgent. I'll come again later.'

'No standing on ceremony. He'll only scold me,' she said, insistent. Futawatari wondered for a moment if she might be serious, if Osakabe really might tell her off.

Why not? I've got nothing to hide.

Futawatari gave his name and title and bowed formally, crossing the door with the feeling of a man entering an enemy stronghold. Osakabe's wife led him to a tatami room with a Shinto altar. There was an amulet devoted to the *daimyojin*, the powerful feudal lords. The altar was well looked after, the plain wood flawless and decorated with leaves that were fresh and bright. The panel above the doors carried a scroll of striking calligraphy bearing the words 'Forget not war in times of peace'. A frame on the wall respectfully highlighted the Commandments of Policing: '1. Serve with pride and duty.'

There was no doubting that Osakabe was an officer to the core.

There was a phone, basic, with no concessions to modern functionality, sitting on a small desk next to the wall. The white spot, untouched by the sun, next to it, would be all that remained of the internal line. Futawatari tried to imagine the number of times Osakabe would have run to it in the middle of a case.

He let out a gentle sigh.

Osakabe's wife had not reappeared since she brought him tea. Under normal circumstances, this behaviour would have come across as cold but, given his current state of mind, he was, if anything, grateful. She had no doubt seen all kinds of visitors during her husband's time in the force. She would have realised from the start that his was not a casual visit.

How should I broach the subject?

Futawatari had been sitting, breathing quietly, for close to half an hour when he heard a car door shut outside. Osakabe's wife came in, as though on cue, and told him her husband was back. Futawatari sat up straight and brought his knees formally together.

No backing down.

But Osakabe did not come in. It was, instead, his wife.

'Sorry, I think he's doing something with the car.'

She craned her neck to indicate a space beyond one of the hedges. Futawatari got to his feet and peered out. Michio Osakabe was standing in view, on the road behind the photinia. The angular features, the eyes like hollows, the glowering profile. They were all unchanged from his time as a detective, emotionless, held in a state that was somewhere between a smile and a frown. Futawatari stepped unconsciously back.

It was as though he'd stumbled across a natural predator.

Osakabe was issuing instructions to the driver, who, except for his grey-speckled hair, remained out of sight. Judging by the noise, they were changing the tyres.

Shit.

It dawned on Futawatari that he could no longer sit and wait. Now he knew that Osakabe was outside, it would be rude to stay in the guest room drinking tea. He bowed his head to Osakabe's wife and started towards the front door, guessing he'd already lost the mind game. Coming to the end of the short hallway, he noticed a collection of traditionally wrapped wedding gifts in a darkened room. Which meant . . . Osakabe's youngest must be getting married. He would have to arrange an official gift from the force, make sure the department heads prepared messages to be read at the reception. Current situation notwithstanding, Futawatari's thoughts returned briefly to procedure.

Outside, the black sedan was raised on a jack, the driver crouched down with a wrench. Osakabe was standing like a rock to the side.

Imperial.

It was rare for a man to truly fit such an old word.

'Sir. It's good to see you.'

Coming to a stop, Futawatari bowed from the waist. *Sir.* He'd used the word without even thinking. Anything less would have been presumptuous. Similarly, he couldn't refer to the man as *Director*, as that might be taken as affirmation of his current position. Futawatari was here to make sure the man stepped down.

The impassive features came around.

'I guessed it'd be you.'

It was the tone Osakabe reserved, without exception, for those who ranked below him. Futawatari had been thirty the first time he'd been on the receiving end. Too accustomed to the courtesies of life in Administrative Affairs, it had struck him like a physical blow. But it wasn't the tone, heard now for the first time in years, which gave Futawatari pause. *I guessed it'd be you.* Those were the words he'd used. That the executive would run and hide. That they'd send Futawatari, who, in his second year as superintendent, was, from Osakabe's perspective, nothing more than a newborn chick.

He'd known it would happen.

Osakabe's back was already turned, as though to say their business was concluded. The driver was fitting the car with winter tyres. They would leave at six in the morning, go deep into the mountains, inspect a site that was still covered in snow. That was all Futawatari had managed to pick up from listening in to their conversation. Having lost his momentum, he stepped back and watched the work continue. He saw a tall stack of road maps on the car's back seat. The number seemed excessive, reminding him of the map he'd seen at lunchtime.

It was only after the driver had finished fitting the tyres, given Osakabe a deep bow and Futawatari a polite nod and left that Osakabe finally turned around. With his feet planted firmly, he levelled his gaze on Futawatari. He had, it seemed, no intention of inviting Futawatari in. *Come on, then. Say it.* The words were there on Osakabe's face.

It wasn't something to discuss in the open, but Futawatari realised he had no choice in the matter. He swallowed some spit and worried that Osakabe might have heard.

'Sir. We need to know what you're thinking,' Futawatari said, having to force his throat to stay open.

Osakabe said nothing.

'Director Kudo will have nowhere to go.' This was something he'd prepared. Kudo was three years Osakabe's junior and Osakabe had always looked out for him.

Still no visible reaction. The man's sunken eyes were

unmoving, trained on Futawatari as though he were taking stock of something.

'Sir, this is a problem.'

' . . . '

'The force will lose face.' This was another one he'd planned, the equivalent of going for the jugular.

Osakabe opened his mouth to speak. 'There's no need to worry.'

'Sir?'

Futawatari wasn't sure what he had meant but he saw a glimmer of hope.

'It'll be like nothing ever happened.'

'I . . .'

'I'm telling you there's no need to get flustered. Once this is done, it'll be like nothing ever happened.' Having said this, Osakabe turned away.

Futawatari understood only that the hope was gone. That it had, in fact, never existed. He scrambled after Osakabe. 'Sir. Why are you refusing to—'

Osakabe turned around, utterly calm. 'It's none of your concern.'

The door slammed shut, leaving Futawatari's hand hanging in mid-air. *It's none of your concern.* Who was he talking about? Administration? The force? To Osakabe, the force was like a mother. Why would he seek to make it an enemy?

The porch light was turned off.

Try as he might, Futawatari could not muster the courage to push the buzzer.

5

And don't bother coming back.

The unhappy childhood memory – of being caught stealing from his father's wallet, of being pushed out of the front door – resurfaced. Administration felt far away. Osakabe had treated him like a kid on an errand. He had spoken in riddles and thrown up a smokescreen. Futawatari had left without the slightest understanding of what the man was thinking.

He raced down the pitch-black of the prefectural highway. His plan was to visit W Block and Yasuo Maejima, one of his contemporaries. *Maejima knows Osakabe.* Anything would do. He just needed something he could use as leverage. He understood that he was acting on impulse but his indignation kept him going regardless.

W Block was a four-storey building containing police apartments. Its name derived from the fact that it accommodated executives from Station W. Whereas the area had previously hosted four executive bungalows, a project to make better use of the land had resulted in the construction last spring of the new complex, which had capacity to house sixteen families.

Maejima gave Futawatari a warm, enthusiastic greeting. It was before seven, but he was already in checked pyjamas and reeking of the hair oil he used after showering. As division chief of Criminal Investigations in Station W, it was something of a miracle for him to be home this early, but it hadn't been intuition alone that had allowed Futawatari to catch him in this rare moment of downtime. He'd called ahead to check, loath to wait yet one more time for someone to arrive home. *Don't worry, it's not business.* Futawatari had made sure to emphasise this before hanging up.

'Come on in. It's nice and quiet inside.'

Maejima was alone; he explained to Futawatari that his wife and kids were out visiting the family home. It seemed a little odd, considering it was his wife who had answered the phone only five minutes earlier, but it was, if anything, a welcome development. Osakabe had acted as a go-between for the couple. Maejima's wife would want to listen in if she heard the name in conversation.

The apartment was the standard layout for police accommodation. In the corner of the tatami room, which became a bedroom at night, was a brand-new desk that looked as though it had just been delivered. There was a glossy black satchel hanging from a hook on the wall. It dawned on Futawatari that the eldest of Maejima's kids, the 'little one' he always talked about, must be ready to start school. It made sense, Futawatari supposed. It had been a few years since he'd received the card announcing another addition to the family. It struck him that he didn't even know whether Maejima still called his eldest 'little one' or not.

'How's things on your side?' Maejima called from the kitchen, then appeared under the *noren* – probably a souvenir from a family trip – with a beer in each hand.

'Same as usual,' Futawatari said, sighing as he refused the glass, saying he couldn't drink but for Maejima to go ahead anyway.

'Black and White still an item?'

Maejima grinned, pouring himself a frothy glass of beer. It was the sort of wisecracking that went on in Criminal Investigations. Futawatari had never heard the joke mentioned in Administrative Affairs, which poked fun at Oguro and Shirota, based on the fact that their names contained, respectively, the characters for black and white.

'Kikyo's mum wants to catch up with you, too, by the way. Complains you're a bit standoffish these days.'

Maejima was as chatty as ever. He skipped from topic to topic, mixing opinion with comic anecdotes, yet never once did he mention any of the cases he was working on. It was impressive. The man had become a stalwart cog in the investigative machine.

It was common for officers who had come through police school together to become like siblings. There was the shared sense of community, the unified sense of purpose. You lived in cramped dorm rooms with little in the way of privacy and submitted yourself to a harsh regimen of training. You comforted one another, shed tears and pledged to keep the peace. Futawatari and Maejima were no exception to the rule. They had since taken their own paths, been separated by rank now Futawatari was superintendent while Maejima was still inspector, yet a single meeting was all it took to take them back to the sweat-infused dorms of the school. The only change was that they no longer discussed work. They'd fallen naturally into this new pattern. And while it brought an increased sense of distance, it felt like nothing more than brothers having become cousins.

'So, you said you'd spoken with the director?' Maejima looked at Futawatari, his face already turning pink. Osakabe had been the man's go-between but he was still 'the director'.

'We had the chance to catch up.'

Maejima leaned in, hungry for more. 'And? How is he?'

'Just the same.'

'I heard he had some problems with his liver last year.'

'Do you visit him?'

'Once or twice a year, sure. Gives me a dressing-down each time. Tells me not to bother, that I need to keep my head focused on work,' Maejima said, chuckling. He seemed to remember something. 'I heard he's going to be staying on at the foundation?'

Caught off guard, Futawatari had to struggle not to choke.

'Where did you hear that?'

'From my wife's cousin. She works there. I think it was last week when she came over and gave us the news. Maybe the week before.'

Maejima would never suspect that this was the reason behind the visit. And news of the arrangements for Kudo to take over upon his retirement from Community Safety would not have reached Criminal Investigations in Station W. Feeling vaguely underhand, Futawatari attempted to pad out the conversation.

'He told me his youngest daughter is getting married.'

'Megu. Right, in June.'

'June. Huh.'

Megu Osakabe. Futawatari had taken notes from Osakabe's file. *Attended a private university. Works for a travel agency in Tokyo. Thirty.* The wedding seemed a little late coming, although Futawatari realised it was no longer uncommon for women to tie the knot in their thirties. There was something else that bugged him, though, about the fact that the wedding was coming up in June. She was Osakabe's youngest. There was no doubt it would be a hugely significant event for the director.

'Will you be going?'

'Absolutely. Wouldn't miss the chance to see Osakabe tear up.'

'Osakabe?'

'He might not look that way, but he dotes on his kids.'

'I can't see it happening. Doesn't seem possible.'

'It'll happen, I guarantee it. He's got a particular soft spot for Megu. She was always a bit delicate. And, well, there was all that other shit that happened.' The casual tone was suddenly gone from Maejima's voice.

'"All that other shit"?'

Maejima blinked, looking shocked as Futawatari quoted the words. 'Yeah, well.'

'What other shit?'

'Anyway . . .' Maejima looked at him as though to suggest he hadn't said a thing.

Futawatari held the man's gaze for a moment then averted his eyes and reached for a handful of peanuts. He knew he couldn't outstare a detective, but his mind was racing. Could this have something to do with the man's daughter? A new scenario unfolded in his mind. Her wedding – Osakabe's youngest daughter's wedding – was coming up in June. Could it be that he simply wished to hold on to his title of managing director until afterwards?

As far as reasons went, it seemed ridiculous. Osakabe's stepping down would have no impact on the fact that he'd been director of Criminal Investigations and managing director of the foundation. He could stand tall as he fulfilled his role as father of the bride.

Futawatari realised, of course, that this was his own objective viewpoint, insufficient, perhaps, to give any insight into the workings of a man like Osakabe, who had devoted himself so completely to his career.

Futawatari's father had been the same. A typical example of the fiercely committed salaryman, he had launched himself headfirst through the years of rapid economic growth, destroying his stomach and liver in the process. His had been a protracted suffering. He had lost his job, become withdrawn, grown old. The one ritual he maintained was that of browsing the classifieds in the morning paper. Futawatari remembered hurrying home after his graduation from police school. *You don't need to worry about me any more. I can look after myself now.* He'd planned the words for his father but his mother had beaten him to it. *Darling, Shinji did it. He's going to be a fully-fledged member of society.* His father hadn't so much as grinned. *And where does that leave me?* His eyes had clouded under a mix of bitterness and envy of his own son. It was the moment Futawatari came to see clearly the flaws of man. The moment he pledged never to let himself become like that.

There was something in Osakabe that reminded him of his departed father. It was part of the reason behind his antipathy for the man.

There was, perhaps, a part of the man's sentiment that was understandable. Osakabe's interest was not in the title, nor was it in having gainful employment. His focus was on being in active service. His insistence on staying on made sense, at least in that context, and particularly with the upcoming wedding complicating matters. Getting married at thirty was late, whatever the current trend. Something had happened to Megu and this had brought about the delay. When the subject was a young unmarried woman, there were, Futawatari suspected, very few scenarios that could be summed up in the way Maejima had expressed it. All of them involved a man, and all ended in tears.

Megu was Osakabe's most cherished daughter. She'd suffered and was now finally on the verge of attaining happiness. Overwhelmed with emotion, Osakabe wanted to give her the best celebration possible. He would stand proud, in active service, as he guided her through her special day.

Futawatari's throat was dry. It was possible he was on the

wrong track. Yet Osakabe had himself said the words only two hours earlier. *It's none of your concern.* Had he wanted to say it didn't concern the force? That it was, instead, a family matter? That – because she'd gone through hell – it was all for Megu?

Could the wife of an officer ever be happy? The question was one Futawatari had decided to ignore. He lacked the courage to ask it of his wife, who lived under the constant scrutiny of those inside and outside the force, who had given her life to him *and* the closed-off community, where the claustrophobia could push you over the edge. That was why the wish was there: *At least, for my daughter.* She was in her fifth year of primary school, chest already developing. She would be asleep by now, breathing softly through her metal braces. Futawatari wished her a life free from such constraints, one in which she could explore the world as she saw fit, never knowing the smothering pressure the force had exerted on her parents. He wished for it with all his heart.

'He's a father, too,' Futawatari muttered to himself. For the first time, Osakabe came across as a flesh-and-blood human, as something more substantial than an ogre locked up in the confines of Criminal Investigations.

'Of course,' Maejima said, speaking for the first time since his slip of the tongue, his voice freeing up, cracking a little.

'Still, I'm pretty sure family wasn't a major factor when he was in the force.'

Maejima muttered another 'of course', his tone darkening just a little.

'What was he like when he was director?'

'Glorious.'

'How so?'

'In every way.'

'So, some kind of superman?'

'Pretty much.' Maejima was kind enough to skip the part that said, *Not that anyone from Administrative Affairs would understand.* Instead, he said, 'Here's something: criminals never return to the scene of the crime.'

'What's that? Something he said?'

'Exactly.'

'But they do, don't they?'

'Truth is, they don't. I checked ten years of case history. Not once did the perpetrator go back to the scene of the crime.'

'So he shares this revelation and stuns you all. That it?'

'You're missing the point,' Maejima said, sounding a little worked up. 'You grow up watching detective shows and you're conditioned, like you, to think it's in a perp's nature to return to the crime scene. Now, imagine you've just committed a crime. There's no way in hell you're going back. Why? 'Cause you're scared shitless you'll be caught. Make sense?'

'I suppose so.'

'What he was telling us was that, in our line of work, we can never take anything we know for granted. It's hard to fathom just how much information is leaked to the outside these days. Investigative techniques. Forensics knowledge. There are people out there who have more know-how than us detectives. Osakabe was telling us that we had to let go of our pride, let go of our preconceptions. That only then could we truly call ourselves detectives.'

Encouraged by the drink, Maejima became increasingly talkative. The anecdotes he gave concerning Osakabe were all fascinating. Futawatari realised, noting as he did a twinge of envy, that Maejima had in Osakabe a superior officer whom he adored without question, one whom he could talk about with nothing but respect.

With the vague promise that he'd come again soon, though unsure as to when that might be, Futawatari left the apartment. His chest felt warm as he walked against the cold wind. Gone were the jagged sensations of anger and humiliation from his visit to Osakabe. He'd told himself he'd come here to gain leverage, but it was possible he'd simply wanted to catch up with a friend. Maybe that was the real reason he'd come.

Cutting through the parking area, Futawatari came to a sudden halt. Under the glow of the mercury lamps, he saw a woman's face in the window of an estate car he recognised by the gaudy strips on the side. He saw two small heads bobbing playfully alongside her. Maejima's 'little ones'. The engine was off but there was no sign of anyone getting out. *You sly bastard.* Futawatari turned to face the light coming from Maejima's apartment. The man had asked his family to wait outside. He'd set it up so he could talk in private with Futawatari. It was transfer season. It was only natural that he would want to know what was in store for him. Would he be up for transfer? Would he be staying? Did he need to pack, get ready to move? Did he need to think about which school his kid would attend?

Futawatari's work had consequences.

Perhaps the kids had been taken for a chocolate sundae.

Futawatari put his foot on the accelerator and kept it there, holding his breath until the estate car had disappeared from the rear-view mirror.

6

It didn't take long to find out what had happened to Megu Osakabe.

The next morning Futawatari had paid a visit to the detention facility in the basement of the north building. Shori Sasaki had been marking numbers on a blackboard, checking as he did a note in his hand. His first job every morning was to call around the various district stations and tally up the number of detainees in the prefecture. His desk was covered in papers and the loose sheets of a questionnaire from a human rights organisation demanding information on the nutritional value of the lunches being served in the facility. Judging by the mess, it seemed fair to assume that Sasaki was busy drafting a response.

Futawatari had dragged him to the kiosk in Welfare. There was a recreation area with some round tables towards the back. Futawatari had tried to exercise restraint when raising the subject, but when Sasaki responded he didn't even try to lower his voice.

'That was a case of forcible violation.'

Futawatari was at a loss as to how to respond. *Forcible violation.* He didn't have to be a detective to know immediately what the term signified.

Megu Osakabe had been raped, five years ago, at a campsite in the north of the prefecture. The attack had come when she'd been out gathering wood for a fire. Her fiancé had been at the campsite with her. It was hard to imagine what the two must have gone through after such an event. In the end, the engagement had been called off. This was what Maejima had meant when he'd referred to 'all that other shit'.

Fucking hell.

Futawatari let out a deep sigh. It wasn't that he hadn't considered rape as a possibility, but to have it confirmed like this felt like taking a bullet in the chest.

'Was the offender arrested?' Futawatari asked, trying to maintain his composure.

Sasaki shook his head. 'Nah, the guy wore a stocking on his head. We know he was getting on a bit, but that's about all. Never got any evidence. He didn't even ejaculate.'

Futawatari was starting to feel sick.

If the man had left any fluids, they could have got his blood type, maybe performed a DNA test to bring him in. Futawatari remembered Osakabe's words, relayed to him by Maejima the previous night. Here was a man with the know-how necessary to circumvent current investigative methods and forensics technology, one willing to commit a crime yet keep his most powerful urge in check to evade arrest.

'What did Osakabe do? I can't imagine how he—' Futawatari began, but Sasaki just looked away, snorting as though to say, *How the hell should I know?*

The man had spent a long time working in the prestigious world of Violent Crime. He'd been proud of the work, calling it the key function of Criminal Investigations. He'd been ranked assistant inspector, two levels below his contemporary Futawatari, but he'd worn it as a badge of honour. Then, four years ago, he'd received an abrupt transfer out. To this day he remained convinced that Osakabe had been the man behind the change in his fate.

Sasaki was silent now, sipping at his coffee, his expression that of a man who had, at some point, abandoned any hope for advancement in the force. There were a few like him in every department, men who showed no signs of apprehension during transfer season.

The sound of laughter prompted Futawatari to glance out of the window. A group of officers from Transport walked by, cracking up at something.

Futawatari couldn't stop himself from trying to imagine Osakabe's feelings. His beloved daughter had been raped and the predator was still at large, and this despite the fact that he had himself led the investigation to hunt the bastard down.

Futawatari thought of something, recalling a detail from Osakabe's file. *Five years ago.* That was the year of Osakabe's promotion to director. Which made it the same year as the murder of the female office worker.

Sasaki was getting ready to leave but Futawatari raised a hand to stop him. 'Five years ago. Wasn't that the same year as the murder of the female office worker?'

'Yep. Not that I worked on that one. That was Maejima's team.'

'So Osakabe's daughter was attacked in the same year . . .'

'There were seven cases like it.'

'Seven?'

'Seven cases of rape with no ejaculation. The last one ended in murder.'

'Were they all the same man?'

'No one knows. The perpetrators all wore stockings, so that's a match, but we never got any hard evidence.'

'But it's probable, right? Considering the last one was when the woman was killed. Perhaps she'd seen his face and he ended up killing her. That would have scared him off, convinced him he had to stop.'

'Sure, maybe. But cases are never that simple.'

Futawatari bid the man farewell at the entrance to the north building. Sasaki returned down the stairs towards the dimly lit basement, moving his neck in lethargic circles. He'd discussed the case, showing glimpses of his past as an investigator, yet he'd failed to consider the first question any real detective would have asked: why was someone from Administrative Affairs showing an interest?

Futawatari's mind was racing as he made his way upstairs. He took slow steps, as though putting the brakes on the obvious conclusion.

A case Osakabe had failed to close. A perpetrator who had probably raped his own daughter. Having failed to bring the man to justice, what would someone like Osakabe, with his forty years of experience in Criminal Investigations, seek to do?

The answer had been there right from the start.

Track him down.

Osakabe was still on the case. He was continuing his work as a detective. He would bring the offender in and he would do so before his daughter's wedding in June.

It was clear now why he was refusing to step down. He was making full use of his position in the foundation. His home had been surrounded by photinia, leaving no space to park. Meaning – he didn't own a car. Maybe it was more than that. As a veteran of an age when detectives traditionally used bicycles and motorbikes to get their work done, it was possible he didn't even hold a licence. He couldn't give up the car and chauffeur. He needed them for his investigation, to enable him to spend his days moving unchecked around the prefecture.

Futawatari brought to mind the enormous map from the office of the foundation. The lines and lines and lines of red pencil, all interwoven like capillaries. Was it possible that, instead of representing the work of the foundation, they were actually a record of Osakabe's own private investigation?

Wait . . .

Futawatari came to a stop on the landing. What, specifically, was Osakabe doing? Futawatari's lack of investigative experience made it hard for him to iron out the details. Was he using the pretext of the site inspections to visit the areas where the assaults had taken place? Futawatari was aware that detectives usually made repeated visits to any given crime scene, but it seemed unlikely that such an approach would help Osakabe find anything new, especially now five years had passed. Was he, then, making the rounds between his inspections with a view to gathering more information? Futawatari suspected that this, too, would be a waste of time. A team of over a hundred detectives had worked day and night on each of the cases. And Osakabe had led the investigations in person.

Despite this, they had failed to make an arrest.

What could one man hope to accomplish now?

A pitch-black trail in the mountains. An image of Osakabe, standing alone.

Futawatari climbed the remainder of the stairs, certain that he had now grasped the reason behind the man's refusal to step down. It felt like an overwhelming weight bearing down on his shoulders.

'You're working on it?' Oguro's chair groaned under the director's immense weight. He glared at Futawatari, who was stood sharply to attention. 'What do you mean, you're working on it?'

'Osakabe refuses to comment, sir. All that is clear is that he has no intention of changing his mind.'

'Yes, well, that much is painfully obvious.'

Oguro slammed the business cards he'd been fiddling with down on to the desk. Futawatari caught sight of names representing construction companies next to those of trustees from the foundation. Oguro had summoned them to his office just an hour earlier. *Hold a board meeting, a general meeting, whatever. Force him out.* Oguro had issued his demands, but the attendees had only bowed their heads in apology. They all feared Osakabe. Just three years ago he had stood as director of Criminal Investigations. He had access to all the information Second Division had gathered during his tenure, information that, in many cases, could be reasonably developed into criminal proceedings. Push him the wrong way and the industry could once again be made a testing ground for investigations into corruption. They had looked terrified.

Division Chief Shirota had been out since noon, making the rounds of the prefecture's major food-manufacturing companies. He had been tasked with finding a stop-gap position for Kudo, should the worst happen and their attempts to remove Osakabe come to nothing. *Consultant – something like that – just for a year.* That was his pitch, but the bubble economy was over and it seemed unlikely that the companies would simply acquiesce. Even if he *did* manage to talk them into it, the press would probably notice the change. They had already covered the background to Kudo's transfer. Someone would start sniffing around, ask why Kudo had been sent to the food industry rather than his previously agreed-upon role of managing director at the foundation. It would doubtless end in an article that highlighted discord within the force.

'I want you to fix this,' Oguro wheezed, as though he were coughing up lead. 'We have two more days. Threaten him if necessary. Find a weakness. You cling to him like a fucking squid until he gives in.'

'. . .'

Futawatari understood why it was that Osakabe had to step down. He did not know to whose assessments or referrals it was that he himself owed his current position, but he was under no doubt that he was, at forty-two, a staunch and loyal member of Administrative Affairs. There was more to the force than Criminal Investigations and Public Security. Futawatari had nothing against the other departments per se, but he knew the organisation needed people who could keep them in check, people who could build the organisation's resilience and ensure it sustained itself through the generations.

That was the mission of Administrative Affairs.

If they stumbled, so, too, would the force. One of the absolute requirements behind the organisation's ability to maintain a monolithic front was Administrative Affairs' continual reminder to those sections who dismissed it as a merely clerical function that they, too, were police. And their greatest weapon in this was Personnel. That was why they could not permit the insurrection.

At the same time, Futawatari knew he had no intention of telling Oguro what he'd learned about Megu. Perhaps it was policemen's honour; he couldn't be sure. He had a daughter of his own. That would be part of it. And there was his natural desire to resist. Oguro was the very embodiment of the career officer, the kind who considered their own self-interest above everything else. Osakabe was making trouble, but he was family. Oguro – a distant relative at best – had no right to interfere.

This is our concern.

Once Futawatari had been dismissed, his next move was to check in at the retreat. Uehara was busy at his keyboard, his look of misery gone. The captain had approved the redrafted transfer plans and work had now shifted to phase two: the reshuffling of officers ranked assistant inspector and below.

'Everything's in order?'

Uehara gave a cheerful nod then frowned when he remembered something. 'Sir, how is the *other* issue?'

Show that kind of consideration in battle, and you'll go far.

With this thought in mind, Futawatari left the building and hurried towards the parking area. He would take Osakabe down.

It would mean stripping the man of his armour and taking hold of his beating heart. But Futawatari had made up his mind, and he had a plan.

8

Futawatari waited for close to two hours, having parked on the same patch of open land next to the river.

The black sedan approached, coming through the evening light with the sidelights on. The indicators blinked and it turned into the residential area. The rear lights left a ghosted trail of red in Futawatari's vision.

He got out of his car and walked to the threshold of the houses, concentrating on the road the sedan had gone down.

He'll have the answers.

Presumably the tyres had been changed again, as it took a full twenty minutes for the car to reappear. Futawatari stepped out into the road, bringing it to a halt. Having seen Futawatari only a day earlier, the driver seemed to recognise him immediately. He wound down his window and cocked his head in Futawatari's direction.

'Something the matter?'

Futawatari put on a pained expression and pointed at the road behind him. 'My car died. Look, I'm really sorry, but I don't suppose I could trouble you for a lift to the station?'

The driver glanced in the direction Futawatari had pointed and offered to take a look. Futawatari replied that he was in a bit of a hurry. The driver nodded and motioned towards the back seat.

Good.

The towering stack of road maps was the first thing to catch his attention. There had to be at least twenty. There were urban maps with residential markings, standard road maps, even maps charting mountain areas resembling the type Forestry might use. Futawatari flicked casually through a few of them.

He let out an almost audible groan.

The pages were covered with red. The lines were everywhere, running in all directions, just as they had on the map in the foundation. There were more lines, if anything, covering more detail and more routes.

Futawatari was tempted to study them further but something caused him to look up. His eyes caught the driver's in the rear-view mirror. The man didn't look bothered, but it was clear he wasn't happy. He had timid features. His grey-speckled hair had given Futawatari the initial impression of a man considerably advanced in years but it was possible he was little more than fifty. The man would know Osakabe's routine inside out. Futawatari had the fifteen minutes it would take for them to reach the Prefectural HQ.

He struck up a conversation as soon as they set off.

The driver introduced himself as Aoki and told Futawatari he'd been doing the job for almost a year. He'd been a taxi driver but, at his age, the night shift had begun to take its toll. He'd had a spell driving for Director Miyagi after the man had broken his arm and following this had been invited to drive full-time for the foundation. His daughter's fiancé owned a yakitori bar, and he'd been thinking about helping out there for a while but had decided in the end that driving was all he was good for.

With this, Aoki gave a brief chuckle.

'Surely this is harder work than driving a taxi? It's the director you're driving around, after all,' Futawatari said.

Aoki disagreed, shaking his head. 'It's better. The daytime hours really help.'

'But you have to drive through snow, down mountain roads.'

'I guess.'

'Does the director do anything else, besides inspect the dumping sites?'

'He has conferences, lectures. That sort of thing.'

'That's not what I . . .' Futawatari's only experience of inter-rogation was from when he'd had to question people during his substation days. This wouldn't be easy. He wondered what Maejima would do in a similar situation. Having considered his options, Futawatari opted to go for the direct approach. 'Does he make any private trips between the inspections?'

'Private trips?'

'Does he meet with people, perhaps, do anything to suggest he's looking into something other than the dumping?'

'I . . .'

It was hard to see Aoki's expression. He'd dropped out of sight of the rear-view mirror. 'You know he used to work for the force, right?'

'I found out not long after I started.'

'Do you know what the red lines are for?'

'They're . . . the routes we take. To the dumping sites.'

'The director draws them himself?'

'Yes.'

'Do you know why?'

'Hmm?'

'I mean, some of these go through residential areas, which I assume have nothing to do with dumping. Does he record the routes you take to the conferences, too?'

'. . .'

Aoki was silent. He reappeared in the rear-view mirror, looking pale. *He's been warned not to say anything.* Futawatari was convinced the man was hiding something, but he lacked the skills necessary to prise out the truth. He saw Maejima's broad grin. The lights of the Prefectural HQ were already closing in beyond the windshield.

9

'Sir, we need to talk.'

Futawatari intercepted Osakabe as he was leaving his house the next morning. His car had just arrived. Aoki seemed to stiffen as he caught sight of Futawatari, no doubt recalling the events of the previous day. Osakabe showed no reaction. He continued impassively towards the car, slipping into the back seat when Aoki smartly opened the door.

Futawatari rushed over and dropped his voice to a whisper. 'I think I understand what you're trying to do.'

Everything hung on the words. Futawatari knew he was close to understanding Osakabe's motivations, yet he had nothing conclusive. He'd gained nothing from his conversation with Aoki and time was almost up. The deadline for notification of the transfers for officers ranked inspector and above was now only a day away.

Please.

For the first time, Osakabe reacted. He focused his gaze on Futawatari, looking like he was weighing things up. He held eye contact for some time.

'Get in.'

Futawatari bowed deeply then hurried into the passenger seat.

'What do you want to say?' Osakabe asked soon after they pulled out.

Futawatari nodded in Aoki's direction, so Osakabe would see. There was a pause before Osakabe spoke again: 'It's fine, go ahead.' Futawatari turned around. He had to choose his words carefully.

'I know about the case from five years ago. I know how it affected you. But I want you to know, sir, that we have officers even now who are—'

'Which case?' Osakabe said, cutting in.

'Sir, five years ago, you must—'

'Be specific.'

'The rape and murder of the female office worker.'

Osakabe fell silent. He seemed unflustered but it was clear he was thinking. Perhaps he was trying to gauge the extent of Futawatari's knowledge.

Futawatari realised that raising the subject of Megu might be enough to get Osakabe to open up. Still, he hesitated. They weren't the only ones in the car.

'It'll be over soon,' Osakabe said abruptly.

'Sir?'

'The detectives have what they need.'

'Evidence?'

'A hair. It's all they need. They'll close the case,' Osakabe said. It was as though he was talking to himself.

Futawatari didn't know how to respond. According to Sasaki, nothing had been left behind. Of course, he'd also said he hadn't worked the case, so it was possible that he simply hadn't known about the hair.

More confusing was the fact that Osakabe had suddenly dropped his guard. Why had he revealed case information? Wasn't it in a detective's DNA to maintain confidentiality? There would have to be a reason behind the casual revelation. *I'm not on the case. It's in capable hands.* Was that what he'd wanted to say?

'I assume headquarters will do?' Osakabe said, giving Aoki the instruction before Futawatari had a chance to respond.

Futawatari turned to face the back of the car. 'Sir, I implore you to consider the effect your actions will have on your successor.'

'. . .'

'It's imperative that—'

'. . .' Osakabe shut his eyes.

Futawatari experienced a surge of anger. 'Could you at least tell me how long it is you intend to stay on at the foundation?'

'. . .'

'Would it be until your daughter's . . .' Futawatari swallowed the rest of the sentence. He couldn't bring himself to say it.

Osakabe's eyes remained closed. Aoki's hands, perhaps due to the tension in the car, were trembling on the wheel. It wasn't long before they pulled up to the parking area outside the Prefectural HQ.

Futawatari leaned further in.

'We need to—'

'It's like I already told you. There's no need to worry.'

'But you haven't—'

'We're finished here. I have work to do.'

The car pulled away, leaving Futawatari standing alone. The sense of defeat was absolute. As was the sense of exhaustion. The man was a rock. *I can't get him to budge.* There would be one final opportunity, that evening, when Osakabe arrived home. Futawatari needed something with which to move the unmoveable.

He had to at least try.

He turned away from the headquarters and started down the main road, pulling open the door to a public phone box. He would place a direct call to the district chief of Criminal Investigations, avoiding the switchboard.

'Futawatari. What is it?' Maejima sounded a little taken aback.

'I wanted to ask you something regarding the case you mentioned, the murder of the female office worker.'

Silence. 'Are you in headquarters?'

'I'm in a phone box. No need to worry.'

'Okay, go ahead. Bear in mind there's some things I can't talk about.'

'Is it true you have evidence? A hair?'

Across the line, Futawatari heard Maejima take a sharp intake of breath. 'Who told you about that?'

'Osakabe.'

Maejima sounded genuinely astonished. He asked repeatedly whether Osakabe had really said such a thing.

'So, it's true?'

'Not really.'

'Osakabe was lying?'

'No, I mean, we did have a hair. But we don't any more.'

'Not any more? What do you mean?'

'The sample was broken down. Atomised.' The effect of Osakabe's endorsement was astounding. Maejima began to talk, almost whispering as he broke the detectives' code of secrecy. It was a particular talent of the detective to come across clearly even when talking quietly.

They had recovered a single hair from the woman's clothes, one that belonged neither to her nor to her family. A year later, still lacking any leads as to the identity of the perpetrator, First Division had made a decision. They had sent their only evidence in for analysis. The testing required chemical processing, which would destroy the sample. That was what Maejima had been referring to. Following the test, the hair would be useless.

The risks, then, had been significant. It was the only evidence they had, but the lack of progress – and the resulting lack of suspects – meant it wasn't being put to use. Getting a blood type would at least allow them to tighten the investigative net. They might even get a lead. Those were the official reasons cited when they submitted the sample for testing.

But there had been more to it than that.

Osakabe's retirement had been a contributing factor, albeit an invisible one. Prior to a senior officer's retirement, detectives liked to do all they could to close any cases that were still open. It was all but tradition to make a special effort to mark the departure of a respected officer. Further complicating the matter in this case was the fact that they had believed the murderer responsible for the rape of Osakabe's daughter. Emotion had taken hold and, as a result, First Division had rushed too soon into the process.

The results had been crushing.

They had sacrificed their only sample and all they learned was that the offender was blood-type A, which applied to four out of ten people. The hair was found to have fallen naturally from the man's head. As such, it had lacked the pieces necessary for DNA processing. The analysis had yielded no further information.

'Maybe it would have been too much to ask for something like Rh negative. But AB, at least, right?' Maejima's voice sounded downcast in Futawatari's ear.

Why lie?

Futawatari recalled what Osakabe had said on the way back to headquarters. Why claim to have evidence where none existed? Had it been some kind of bluff? Just another way to deflect Futawatari's questions, more of the man's signature smokescreen? Could the words have carried some other kind of meaning? Thinking about it now, much of what Osakabe had said didn't seem to make sense. Futawatari couldn't even tell if Osakabe had meant what he'd said. It was possible he'd only said whatever he thought necessary to get Futawatari to back off.

Futawatari tipped his head in response to the duty officer's salute as he walked into the Prefectural HQ. He felt physically and mentally heavy. *I can't see tonight going well. Not at this rate.* He had braced himself for the director's rancour upon entering Administration but the office was almost eerily quiet.

Shirota came over and whispered the words, 'Director Kudo has announced he won't be taking the position.'

Futawatari opened his eyes and looked the man in the face. He was grinning.

'Turns out he's been having some health issues.'

'Health issues?'

'Right. Anyway, we're in the clear.'

'A job well done.' A deep voice sounded behind them. Oguro's smile reached all the way to his eyes.

Futawatari felt like he'd fallen into a well. The question of Osakabe's refusal to step down had resolved itself. Just like that, with no harm done.

Don't you see what this means?

He felt the urge to scream the words. Osakabe had intervened and Kudo had followed his bidding, removing Futawatari from the equation.

Laughter came from inside the director's office. Futawatari clenched his hands to extinguish the shame, which now burned more strongly than ever.

10

There's no need to get flustered. Once this is done, it'll be like nothing ever happened.

It was as Osakabe had predicted. The calm in the office seemed to suggest that the whole debacle had never even taken place. Neither Oguro nor Shirota mentioned the subject again. The fruits of Uehara's labour were officially announced and the transfer season quickly passed. The only event of note was when the disgraced captain of Station S came by, dipping his head in gratitude as he made the rounds to thank everyone for his new post as chief of Licensing.

Administration had a transfer of its own. Officer Saito was reassigned to Criminal Investigations in Station W. She had a stubborn streak that belied her appearance, and Futawatari suspected she might give Maejima a run for his money. Futawatari, too, had started to move on. In the weeks and months that followed, the plans to rebuild the headquarters were beginning to come together. He was busy negotiating with the various departments, as well as laying the groundwork in the prefectural assembly, and the memories of Osakabe's face and voice were beginning to fade.

Yet every now and then Futawatari still found himself asking the question.

Is he out there now? Working on the case?

Osakabe had been on his mind in June, too. Someone had told him that Megu had looked stunning in her dress. Maejima had got blind drunk and failed to notice whether Osakabe had actually shed tears. And, despite Futawatari's suspicion that that would be the end, he continued to hear nothing of Osakabe stepping down.

Had the whole thing even happened? As another three months went by, Futawatari could no longer be sure.

He was in a bad mood on the day he found out.

The various departments had been fighting over floor space, causing a delay in putting together the blueprints for the new building. The post-bubble economy was down, too, meaning lower tax revenues, which threw the whole existence of the project into doubt. On top of this, the NPA had made one-sided requests that the Department of Community Safety be renamed the Department of Public Safety and that the Patrol Unit be renamed the Community Unit. They had also suggested that the name of one of the prefecture's dorms, Standby Hall, was too passive and asked that that be changed, too.

And what the hell is wrong with 'Standby Hall'? Isn't that what the police do? Stand by until the shit hits the fan?

Futawatari was venting his frustration on his memo pad, phone under his chin, when a familiar figure walked into his peripheral vision. He drew a sharp breath.

Osakabe.

The man glanced in Futawatari's direction before disappearing into the director's office with Shirota in tow.

Had something happened?

Futawatari's heart was racing; he felt suddenly apprehensive.

Osakabe was in the office for no more than five minutes. When he re-emerged, he left without even sparing Futawatari a look.

Oguro and Shirota watched him go from the side of the office door. Futawatari overheard a quiet, bitter-sounding voice.

'He could have at least apologised for all the fucking trouble.'

Had he agreed to step down?

Futawatari jumped to his feet. He made a beeline through the office and started to jog down the corridor.

Why?

He picked up speed as he made his way down the stairs, leaving the building via the main entrance. Osakabe was already inside the black sedan, which was still in its parking space.

'Sir!'

Futawatari pressed his hands on the window. Osakabe turned to face him.

'Sir. What changed your mind?'

'. . .'

Osakabe's eyes appeared to cloud over. In the next moment he issued an instruction for his driver to pull out. Something seemed out of place.

It . . . isn't Aoki.

In his place sat a young man wearing silver-rimmed glasses. The maps, too, were gone. The back of the car held none of the towering stacks he'd seen before. The car pulled sharply away, as though to emphasise the youth of the new driver.

Futawatari remained where he was. His pulse was pounding in his ears. *The clouded-over look. The new driver. The disappearance of the maps.* The images flashed by in quick succession. The discrete facts began to come together, as though magnetised, joining to form clumps and eventually coalescing into a single realisation that thumped against the inside of his skull.

Impossible.

Futawatari broke into a run, almost knocking over the stunned officer on entrance duty as he made for Media Relations. Apologising to the female officer in the room, he opened the file containing the day's papers and put it on her desk. He scanned the obituaries. The papers all had a section now, hoping it would expand their readership.

Two days. Three days. Four days ago.

Futawatari's eyes opened wide.

There.

He hurried back out of the building. He kept running, aiming for the phone box on the main road, and kept going when he saw it was taken. His hands were shaking when he finally inserted his phone card.

'It's me.'

'You calling from the office?'

'Don't worry, I'm outside.'

'What is it this time?'

'The murder. There's one last thing I need to know.'

'Hey, haven't I already—'

'The colour.'

'Huh?'

'I need to know the colour of the man's hair.'

The transition to autumn was unmistakeable. The neatly trimmed hedges of photinia had grown withered and unattractive. They were, Futawatari supposed, at their best when newly blooming and vividly red.

'Did you get what you wanted?' In the tatami room, under the watch of the Shinto altar, Futawatari's voice was muted.

Osakabe was dressed in traditional attire. He sat with his arms crossed, his sunken eyes fixed on Futawatari.

The sample of hair had been grey. Rather than tell him outright, Maejima had simply named a brand of hair dye.

Genichiro Aoki had died from an overdose of sleeping pills. *Judging by the number he took, I'd say it was probably suicide.* An inspector from Forensic Autopsy, a colleague of Futawatari's from his substation days, had shared his private opinion. The death had occurred not long after the newly wed Megu had returned from her honeymoon. The inspector, head cocked to one side, had seemed puzzled as to why the man would kill himself.

'Sir, you drove him to . . . I guess I played a part, too.'

'. . .'

Osakabe's poker face showed no signs of cracking. Futawatari let out a heavy sigh. Osakabe had found out the truth. All of it.

It had begun with a coincidence.

Aoki had given up his job as a taxi driver, opting instead to take the more comfortable role of driving for the foundation. He would never have expected that he would end up working for a retired police officer. He'd told Futawatari as much, that he'd discovered this only after he'd accepted the job.

Osakabe's curiosity would have been piqued. There were, of course, countless men with greying hair. Yet that would not have stopped him from focusing on one presented to him like this. It was a detective's nature to follow every lead, however remote.

Perhaps their meeting had been more than coincidence. Aoki had driven for Miyagi before his invitation to work for the foundation. It was possible Osakabe had had his eyes on Aoki from the start. If so, he might well have played a part in Aoki's eventual employment.

Whatever the case, it had become Osakabe's routine to watch the man from his place at the back of the sedan. Then, one day, something had caught his attention. Aoki would have avoided taking a particular route. Or perhaps exhibited a subtle change in behaviour when driving past a particular area.

One of the seven assault sites.

Criminals don't return to the scene of the crime. They do all they can to avoid it.

Osakabe would have been sceptical at first. That was why he'd decided to make such an overwhelming number of trips. Miyagi had said that Osakabe had been making his daily excursions for a year. That fitted with the start of Aoki's employment. Osakabe had compelled the man to drive, day after day after day. Through the mountains, through the cities, in every direction. The whole time, Osakabe had been keeping watch, tailing his suspect, staking him out. The assault sites would have been etched in his mind. Which route would Aoki take? When and where would he exhibit a change in behaviour? Observing it all with a keen eye, Osakabe had taken note of the man's every gesture, glance and breath. He'd recorded the details on the enormous map in the foundation and in the stacks of maps in the car. And he'd done it all in front of Aoki so as to gradually dial up the pressure. Chemical analysis had robbed the force of the only evidence they'd had. Intimidation was the only way to close the case. Osakabe would back the man into a corner and force a confession.

That was the conclusion he'd reached.

But a year had gone by and Aoki's guilt had remained in question. Osakabe had failed to turn up anything conclusive. That was when he'd decided to continue the investigation and to stay on at the foundation.

What about Aoki's take on all this?

Shortly after his appointment he had found out that Osakabe had been in the force. He'd have been spooked. Yet he would not have known that Osakabe had led the investigation into the murder, nor that he was the father of one of the victims. It was possible he'd treated the threat lightly. Four years had passed since the last assault and the investigation had never closed in. He'd been careful, too, so as not to get caught. He hadn't ejaculated. He'd worn a stocking to conceal his face and to stop any hairs from going astray. And chauffeuring was preferable to driving a taxi. He didn't want to let the opportunity slip him by. That would doubtless have been part of his thinking.

Approaching one of the assault sites, he would have opted wherever possible for an alternative route. When that wasn't an option he'd have held his breath and driven straight on. Osakabe had been using maps to keep track of their routes. Aoki hadn't known why but, over time, this had given rise to the unpleasant sense that he was being surveilled. He would have considered leaving the job. But his daughter had been due to get married in September the following year. He'd have needed the money. So he'd forced himself to keep going, despite the increasing anxiety. No doubt it had happened something like that.

That was when Futawatari had appeared with his mission to talk Osakabe into giving up his position at the foundation. Osakabe had shunned contact at first, convinced he would only get in the way of his investigation. But Futawatari had persisted. He'd even begun to suspect that Osakabe's desire to stay on was in some way connected to the murder. Osakabe had been forced into making a decision. He could continue his surveillance of Aoki, applying gradual pressure, as before, or he could take a risk and use Futawatari's unscheduled appearance to his advantage.

He'd decided on the latter.

That was why he'd told Futawatari to continue when he'd seen his reluctance to talk in front of Aoki, making sure the subject of the murder came up. His next play had been taboo. He'd told Futawatari the force had a sample, a hair, when none existed. He'd said the case would be closed, and soon. The words had, of course, been for Aoki. And Futawatari's blind stumbling had made him complicit in the entrapment.

Aoki would have been terrified. A retired police officer and an on-duty inspector were discussing a murder that *he'd* committed. Osakabe was also claiming that the force had hard evidence in the form of a hair. That would have panicked Aoki. He'd have thought about leaving the job. But that would only arouse suspicion. He'd have realised that, too. His thoughts would have turned to disappearing. But that would be tantamount to confession. He would become a wanted man, spend the rest of his life on the run. What would become of his wife? Of his daughter and her wedding? He'd spent sleepless night after sleepless night.

With each passing day, he'd increased the dosage of his sleeping pills. He'd have been haunted by images of Osakabe. By those sunken eyes, unwavering, fixated on his back.

The eyes that were now trained on Futawatari, their only purpose, it seemed, to dig into a man's soul. They had watched Aoki relentlessly for the six months following Futawatari's return to everyday life in Administration.

But was that all that Osakabe had done? There was one more question Futawatari felt he had to ask.

Osakabe's wife came in with tea and knelt on the floor to serve it. She would not, Futawatari knew, reappear until it was time for him to leave. He waited for her footsteps to fade before he broke the silence.

'Did you get a confession?'

'. . .'

'Did he admit to his crimes?'

Osakabe closed his eyes. He sat like that for some time. Futawatari sighed. Warm afternoon sunlight bounced off the water in the ashtray, flickering over the sliding doors.

'What do you intend to do now?'

Futawatari had meant to ask two questions with this. *What will you do after the foundation?* And: *What will you do to process all that's happened?*

'Sir, Aoki is dead.'

'. . .'

'The bastard's dead. There's nothing more you can do.'

'No,' Osakabe whispered.

'Sir?'

'Maybe the bastard's dead. The moment you say that is the moment you're done as a detective.'

'. . .'

'The bastard's out there, having the time of his life. That's what we're here for. Understand?' Osakabe closed his eyes again. He might have been asleep, except there was no peace in his expression.

He hadn't heard Aoki confess. Futawatari was sure of it now. Which meant that the man would live on, his guilt never proven.

It was time to leave.

Osakabe's wife saw Futawatari to the door, remaining in a deep bow until he had disappeared from view. He walked to the patch of open land next to the river.

Osakabe would not celebrate Aoki's death. Despite his conviction that Aoki was the culprit, he had not requested a background check. He'd had Megu to consider. She was newly married, finally happy. News of an arrest would only drag her back into the nightmares of the past. Not wanting that, he would have perhaps chosen to run the man into a corner, force him into taking his own life. Perhaps that had been his plan all along. It was one he wouldn't forgive himself for. Get the bastards in cuffs – that was the duty of a detective.

Futawatari gazed up at a clear sky. The cost projections for the new helicopter would be on his desk in Administration. Their pilot was getting old. Perhaps, for the next one, they could train up someone in the force. Still, the safe bet was probably to arrange another transfer from the self-defence forces.

He stretched up, reaching for the blue.

Maybe I'll pay Maejima's ugly mug a visit, once today's done.

He remembered something. Hurrying back to the car, he began to rummage through his overstuffed briefcase. It was in there somewhere; it had to be. Forgotten until now, he looked for the gift his wife had given him six months earlier to celebrate Maejima's eldest starting school.

CRY OF THE EARTH

Yamamoto declared over the FM radio that the weather wouldn't last; that, come evening, there would be rain. Takayoshi Shindo glanced up and saw heavy clouds in the distance. Arranged like a recumbent Buddha, they obscured the strikingly beautiful line of the mountains, muddying the colours that stretched from the hills to the peaks.

But it was the time, more than the weather or the view, that was dominating Shindo's thoughts as he sat with his hands on the wheel. He had hoped to be back at the headquarters by three. The routine check-up following his operation to remove a stomach ulcer had taken longer than expected. The main building was already visible up ahead, yet construction work and a closed lane meant traffic was moving at a slow crawl.

Despite all this, he managed to pull into the officers' parking area as his watch, set a few minutes fast, changed to three o'clock. He climbed the gravel slope, jogged across the city road and was just passing behind the garage used by Transport's mobile unit when the familiar music came into earshot.

The daily exercises, funnelled over the crackle of the building's tannoy.

It was a time of day when the officers of the Prefectural HQ allowed their stern expressions to relax. Some slumped back in their chairs, dispensing eyedrops into bloodshot eyes. Others swayed in time to the music, moving flabby waists. A female officer clutching a bright-red purse gave Shindo an abbreviated bow as she hurried downstairs, shoes clicking loudly. Perhaps the stall in Welfare had been restocked with sweets.

Three in the afternoon. It was a time of day Shindo had always enjoyed – until this year, and until he had turned fifty. It had been six years since his promotion to superintendent and, if all had gone to plan, he would have been appointed captain of a small district station in the spring. Instead, he had coughed up blood just before the transfers were due. *Hospitalisation. Operation. Recuperation.* The amended details of his transfer had been delivered to him while he was in bed at home. *Inspector, Internal Affairs Division, Department of Administrative Affairs.* He had started the post a month behind schedule. Ever since, the time of day had become a bleak reminder of what might have been.

It was also the time when, every day, the bike carrying the day's post would roll up to the main entrance.

Shindo pushed on the rust-coloured door and walked into Internal Affairs, not quite blending in with the calm around him. At the chief's desk at the back of the room, a pair of white gloves were in motion.

They'd had post today, too.

'Sorry. The tests took a bit longer than expected.'

Division Chief Takegami peered up in brief acknowledgement, but his eyes fell quickly back to the letter in his hands. The light reflecting in his glasses made it hard to read his expression. Shindo made a quick scan of the desk.

Five letters.

The first to catch his attention was an envelope with an address written in oversized characters. *Captain, Prefecture D Police*

Headquarters. Judging by the shoddy penmanship, it was probably the usual from the butcher. Each week the man sent a list of complaints, bemoaning traffic management or the lack of patrols in the commercial shopping district. An 'under consideration' would suffice for him. That left four more.

Takegami's examination of the letter looked as though it would take a while longer.

I'll get on with my work.

Shindo turned the key to his locker and extracted the bunch of papers relating to commendations and disciplinary actions. Information on both were collected here, in Internal Affairs.

Commendations were fine.

For someone who had made a significant contribution to closing a case, there were accolades such as the Captain's or Director's Trophy, awarded by the Prefectural HQ and National Police Agency respectively. It was in his remit to congratulate the general workforce for their tireless labour, too, those who engaged day and night in work that was far from glamorous. He could cast a spotlight, say, on the young married couple who had watched over a snow-blasted parking area in the middle of nowhere.

As a fellow officer of the law, it was work that felt good. It was the disciplinary side which was a challenge.

The majority of the force saw the primary role of Internal Affairs as being to sniff out and investigate inappropriate behaviour then assign the appropriate penalty. Shindo had been no different.

Fucking spies.

He'd said things like that in the past. Now, he was one of them.

'Shindo!' Takegami called out, removing his glasses.

Here we go.

Shindo donned a pair of white gloves and approached the chief's desk. As was usual, Takegami had sorted the letters into groups. Three to the left. One in the middle. One more to the right.

'I think the first three can be safely dismissed. The one in the middle claims that an officer from Station W got a bit rough handling a drunk. I think I'll get Katsumata to check that out. Now, this last one . . .' Takegami motioned his chin towards the letter on the right. 'I'd like you to take a look at it.'

Shindo took the letter and returned to his desk. First was the envelope. The address read: *Internel Affairs, Prefecture D Police Headquarters*. The characters were oddly flat on the bottom, suggesting the use of a ruler. The postmark belonged to the central sorting office in City P, which was under the jurisdiction of Station Q in the south. Shindo turned the envelope over. There was nothing to indicate the sender.

It's a tip-off.

Shindo took a breath before he inspected the contents. A single sheet of A4. The paper was glossy, the kind used with word processors. The characters were . . . yes . . . printed. The content was spaced over three rows:

Division Chief of Public Safety, Station Q
Seeing Proprietress of Mumu
Hotel 6 9

Division Chief of Public Safety, Station Q . . .

Shindo was unable to immediately put a name to the position. This was partly due to the fact that he'd been in hospital during the last set of transfers but also because his history was in Security, as a member of the riot police and as a bodyguard for key personnel. As such, his knowledge of Public Safety was limited, at best. Even then, the blip lasted only a few seconds.

Yoshio Sone.

The memories flowed in. The man's name, his face, even the mocking jingle he was known for: *Sone, Sone. Hmm, hmm, always hmm.* The tune, sung behind the man's back, played in his head, as clear as ever. *Should we bring the bastard in? Hmm, hmm, hmm. Should we let him go? Hmm, hmm, hmm.*

Always running to the captain for help. Guy isn't cut out for the job. It was the bitter conclusion drawn by each and every one of his juniors. Back when Shindo had been ranked inspector, he'd spent a year in the same district station as the man. Shindo had been chief of Security, while Sone had been chief of Community Safety, the name of which had been changed, this year, to Public Safety. Five years Shindo's senior, Sone would be fifty-five. When his name came up these days it was no longer in reference to the jingle but to the length of time he'd spent as inspector. At seventeen years and counting, his term was the longest in the prefecture.

'Well? What do you think?'

Takegami came into view. He wasn't asking for Shindo's opinion on the content of the letter. Three lines was insufficient to furnish a sense of whether the claim was genuine. That would take more work. For now, Takegami was asking for Shindo's take on the source.

Was the informant someone in the police? Or someone on the outside?

If it was the latter, of course, that would present its own kind of problem. They would need to track the informant down and find a way to defuse the situation. If it was someone who was involved with the proprietress – the *mama-san* – someone who had grown jealous and sent the letter in, then Internal Affairs would have no choice but to intervene and sort out the mess. Such situations could not be allowed to fester, in case they became violent. And should the information ever go public, the fallout would not stop at Sone. The force itself would take a hit.

The more worrying scenario, however, particularly when it came to safeguarding the interests of the force, was that in which the informant was a member of the police force. Internal Affairs was more than ready to hear out work-related grievances, but to hide in anonymity and seek to discredit a colleague or a senior officer . . . that kind of behaviour was nothing short of contemptuous and could not be tolerated. There was a greater risk of the media becoming involved, too. Internal informants liked to hide in the shadows and keep an eye on the actions of Internal Affairs. Should things not go to plan, they would invariably leak the story to the press. They were the enemy within and they deserved the greatest censure the force could levy.

Shindo examined the letter one last time. He saw nothing to override his gut feeling. The informant was someone on the inside.

There was the fact that the letter was only three lines long. Outside informants tended to write line after line of invective, spilling their rage until it had abated. Furthermore, as there was nothing in the letter to suggest blackmail, someone on the outside would have had no real reason to use a word processor or a ruler to disguise their handwriting. The address, too, had contained an error in the spelling: 'Internel' instead of 'Internal'. The existence of the division was not common knowledge outside the force and, if someone had looked it up, it seemed unlikely they'd have made such a basic mistake.

'It's a rat.'

Takegami responded with a firm nod, signalling his agreement. 'Do me a favour and look into it.'

Shindo got up from his seat. He took two copies of the document and put them in his drawer, then left the room with the original in a plastic sleeve. He passed Senior Inspector Masanori Katsumata on the way. The man's goggle eyes stood out against his golf tan.

'Anything big today?'

'Nothing special,' Shindo answered, keeping it vague as he headed for the stairs.

He couldn't let Katsumata catch wind of the letter. The appearance of an inspector from Internal Affairs always brought a certain level of tension, regardless of the division in question. Katsumata relished the feeling and had developed a tendency of making the rounds even when he had no official business. He liked to gossip and thrived on being the centre of attention. If he chanced on someone he knew, there was the risk he would get carried away and mouth off about the content of the letter. There was evidence, Shindo knew, to suggest that this had happened in the past.

Katsumata was not the kind of man you posted to a place like Internal Affairs.

There was nothing to prove Sone's misconduct and yet Shindo knew that word of the letter would be enough to end Sone's career. A vague image came to mind of the man standing to attention, in uniform, his face flushed red.

He's not a bad man, that much is certain.

With the three o'clock period of calm over, the mood in the headquarters felt endlessly grim.

2

Shindo's first step was to visit the crime lab on the fourth floor of the main building.

He requested that Assistant Chief Mizutani test the letter for prints, enquiring at the same time whether it might be possible to deduce the model of word processor from the font. Mizutani had muttered that he'd give it a shot, the sort of clipped response that was typical of officers with a technical background. Shindo was fine with that. The lab was essentially a hive of scientists. They could spend the whole night peering through microscopes, examining each and every character in the letter, yet they would never once show any interest in the meaning contained within it. Theirs was a world far removed from anything as commonplace as gossip.

Next on his list was Forensics.

Tests like these were usually routed through Forensics, so Shindo thought it better to inform Division Chief Mitsuo Morishima that he'd gone straight to the crime lab. Back in his substation days, Shindo had kept an eye out for the man, who'd been a new recruit at the time. He was a coarse man, but he gave a sharp nod at the courtesy, indicating he would probably refrain from poking his nose into it.

It's too easy to kill a man with a rumour.

Shindo considered this as he headed back downstairs.

The prefecture was scheduled to host a number of major sporting events in the coming spring, each of which warranted a visit from the Imperial Family. In order to avoid any issues with security, the transfer season was to be moved forward. It was probably safe to assume that the groundwork was already underway, even though it was only autumn. If rumours of Sone being involved in an improper relationship were to surface now, at this key time, he'd probably remain inspector until his last day in the force.

Police inspectors are undoubtedly the heroes of fiction. Armed with brains *and* muscle, they are the face of the organisation, as they occupy the front lines. In many ways the image is accurate, the only difference being that, in real life, inspectors grow old. Those who make the rank at a young age naturally set their sights on becoming superintendent. The transition is necessary for anyone who wishes to approach the inner circle of the force, giving them more troops to lead and affording more opportunities to spearhead real change. It is only after you make superintendent, for example, that executive positions such as captain in district, or division chief in the Prefectural HQ, become available.

And yet, after seventeen years, Sone was still struggling to close the book on his chapter as inspector.

In Prefecture D, promotion to superintendent depended on a mix of performance reviews, interviews and exams. Length of service was also taken into account, meaning the older inspectors were, generally speaking, the first in line for promotion. Yet none of this was set in stone. The executive had the final say in who they moved up, and the number of officers waiting their turn was always greater than the number of posts available. This led to the gradual emergence of people like Sone, who, overtaken by their juniors, might wait ten or even fifteen years and still not hear the 'call from above'.

There were, of course, those who had been held back for past indiscretions. Yet in the majority of cases there was nothing wrong with the officers themselves. They may not have had the right manager to pull them up. They may have had the right skillset but lacked ambition. Been unlucky enough to have a group of exceptional officers below them. Luck could play a significant role. Sure, Sone had been criticised for his failings as a leader, but a quick look around revealed superintendents who were no different. And he didn't even scratch the surface when it came to currying favour to get ahead. There were superintendents now lounging in key positions who were completely without shame in that regard.

All things being equal, inspectors constituted a group which had already navigated their way through a number of exams and declared their intention to aim for the top. It wasn't easy, should your path to superintendent be delayed, to take a step back and argue the case for spending the rest of your career in the field. All that remained for those stuck in their position was a slow, creeping anxiety.

There *were* calls for the prefecture to introduce, over the next couple of years, a written exam for officers trying for superintendent. Yet even this would be of little help to the veteran inspectors. If anything, it threatened to worsen their situation. Immersed in the daily grind, they would have spent close to a decade away from exams. They would find it hard to summon the energy needed to outperform their younger peers, all of whom were capable and ambitious in their race up the ladder.

That left the upcoming spring. The next round of transfers would be Sone's last chance for promotion before the deployment of the new exam. He would be waiting with bated breath, hoping for the call from above. It would perhaps be a miracle, considering he'd never even held a vice-captain's post in district. Still, it wasn't unheard of for Personnel to grant a promotion out of charity. The man still had a greater-than-zero chance of making it.

But someone was trying to reduce even that to nothing. Maybe someone he had worked with, someone who held a grudge of some kind.

Shindo's hand shot to his abdomen. Ever since he'd lost half his stomach, the remainder had taken to expressing his anger.

If you're going to hang someone, at least do it to someone more deserving. Someone with more clout.

It was true that Sone lacked what it took to lead. That he wasn't, perhaps, a natural fit for a role in management. Yet the man Shindo knew had never looked down on others. He'd always been the first to arrive at work and the last still hunched over his desk at night. He'd never sought to gain from his status as an officer of the law. Shindo remembered a time when Sone had spent hours listening to a woman talk about her runaway son, all the while interjecting his signature *hmm, hmm, hmm.* Shindo was struck by a thought. Wasn't Sone, in that image, the very embodiment of a decent and hard-working member of the force?

Despite this, the informant was mocking him. Sneering, even as Sone waited, anxiously praying for his last shot at promotion, humming his tune in the dark.

It was, of course, possible that Sone *had* become involved with the *mama-san*, that Shindo's impression was wide of the mark. It was possible that Sone had long ago abandoned any hope of promotion, that he'd lost sight of his former integrity. The man worked for Public Safety, too, which looked after the licensing of bars and other such venues. He would have contacts. What if he'd sought to take advantage of his status as chief to make a move?

Shindo left the main building.

He headed down the city road and walked into the Prefecture

D Mutual Funds Association, which was located alongside the headquarters. As an affiliated organisation, many of the senior positions were occupied by officers who'd retired from the force. Shindo bowed to familiar faces as he requested an off-the-record appraisal of Sone's accounts. If the claims were true, he would need money.

Nothing came up.

Sone had taken out a single loan of one million yen to help finance the purchase of a car. That was three years ago, and it had already been repaid in full. The man's finances were clean. Still, there was no shortage of alternatives for securing money, particularly if your preference was for secrecy. The fact that Sone had a clean record with the association did not in itself prove that all was in order. Nonetheless, Shindo breathed a sigh of relief. If anything had been flagged at this stage, he would have had no choice but to consider more seriously the possibility of Sone's guilt.

There was a note on his desk when he got back to Internal Affairs. He waited until Katsumata was out then put in a call to the crime lab.

'No prints.'

Mizutani's clinical tone was all the more jarring over the phone, but Shindo was not disappointed to hear the result. It was what he had expected. Shindo thanked him and requested that he call again if they managed to work out the model of the word processor. He hung up.

That leaves tonight.

Shindo opened the commendations file. At the same time, he considered his assets in Station Q. *Who should I use?* Sorting through his options, he winced a little as the word 'spies' flashed into his mind.

3

Shindo had dinner at a noodle bar near headquarters, one popular with the motorbike units for takeaways. He'd heard they served a good meal that didn't weigh too heavily in the stomach. No doubt this was an important consideration for the mobile squads, whose insides were constantly being churned up by the exposed engines of their bikes. For Shindo, who lacked half a stomach, the tip seemed too good to pass up.

It was dark by the time he had finished, still not raining. Shindo suspected that Yamamoto would be getting more than a little peeved by now.

The police apartments were five minutes away by car. On the second floor, room eight was completely dark. Turning his key in the door, Shindo came to a sharp halt when he sensed something move in the room. *It's just the fax machine.* He flicked on the lights to see a sheet of paper with handwriting on it he recognised – characters slanted upwards and to the right – slide into view.

I hope work was okay. How was the check-up? Akiko is studying hard. We got the results of her mocks. She was placed fifty-six out of a thousand!
    Love, Kanako

His wife's current obsession was to get their daughter through her university entrance exams. She spent half the week at the apartment in Tokyo, helping her while she attended cram school. *Why did it have to be English lit?* The two of them shared a passion he simply couldn't understand, however much he tried. He waited for the buzz that signalled the end of the transmission then picked up the receiver.

Kazuki Yanagi.

That was who he had decided to use. *Police sergeant, Criminal Investigations, Station Q. Thirty-two. Single.* Yanagi had worked under him for two years back when he'd been sub-leader in the riot police. The man's work was impeccable; he was level-headed and utterly reliable. More importantly, he was like a clam in his ability to keep a secret.

Yanagi's sister answered. The two had lost their parents while they were still young and Yanagi was currently letting her bunk in his room in the Station Q dorms while she studied at technical college. It was only seven o'clock, so it was no surprise to hear he was still out. Shindo asked if she would get Yanagi to return his call when he got back, whatever the hour; he then enquired whether she knew if her brother owned a fax machine. She sounded puzzled when she told him she didn't think so.

Shindo ended the call. Receiver still in hand, he punched in the number of an electronics shop that was owned by an old acquaintance. He told the man he wanted a fax installed in Yanagi's room first thing in the morning, adding that the delivery had to be discreet. It wasn't the first time he'd made such a request, so the man readily agreed, saying he'd take it in a box for a vacuum cleaner, something like that.

Good.

Shindo took out the city map and phone book that he'd brought from the office and opened them on the table. First was the bar: Mumu. He flicked through the directory and quickly found it. He'd guessed the characters would read as 'Mumu' and the index confirmed that this was the case. He took note of the address and slid his finger over the map. *There*. Right in the middle of the red-light district. Next was Hotel 69, City P. *Yep*. He caught sight of the name on the map. It was around five kilometres west of the bar, straight along the city road. It appeared to fall under the jurisdiction of Station F, just beyond that of Station Q. In the informant's letter, the numbers six and nine had been printed with a space between them, yet no such gap existed in the phone book or on the map, meaning it had probably been a typo.

Shindo felt a little bothered by the fact that the bar and hotel had turned out to be real. The letter seemed all the more credible for it. And it didn't help that the hotel was under the jurisdiction of Station F. *If you're going to meet someone, make sure it's outside your territory.* It was a textbook move, and that was why he didn't like it.

It was after ten when Yanagi called.

'Sir, it's been a while.'

The words were polite enough, but the man's tone was flat, hinting neither at nostalgia for an old boss nor concern that the call had come out of the blue. His was a coolness designed to keep others at a distance, a world apart from the clinical indifference of the officers in the crime lab. It was exactly why Shindo considered him a perfect fit for this kind of investigation.

Telling him first that this was to remain private, Shindo went on to outline the content of the letter.

'That's what we've got. Can you think of anyone who might have something against Sone?'

'I can think of two people. The first . . .'

Shindo was caught unprepared. Stopping Yanagi mid-sentence, he searched for something to write on. 'Okay, go ahead.'

'The first . . . would be Toshio Saga.'

Shindo scribbled the details on the back of a leaflet. *Toshio Saga. Forty-three. Police sergeant. Public Safety Division, Juvenile Section. Station Q.* The man lived with his mother, who was frail and essentially bedridden. Personnel had treated him exceptionally well and had allowed him to stay in Station Q for twenty years. He had been through most of the divisions and, two years ago, had been posted to Public Safety. According to Yanagi, the man hardly spoke to Sone. If anything, he had been openly hostile since the latter's transfer one year ago. Having a reputation for being a troublemaker, it wasn't unthinkable that he would take action to get rid of someone he didn't like.

'The second . . . would be—'

Atsushi Mitsui. Thirty-four. Public Safety Section. Patrol officer. Sone had given Mitsui the task of setting up a crime-prevention committee and told him to sell the idea to the landlords. The aim was to improve the vetting process for tenants moving into the station's jurisdiction. The landlords, however, worried that additional checks would steer potential tenants away, were unwilling to cooperate. Struggling to get the project going, Mitsui was beginning to crack under the stress. The man was already a bit of a laughing stock, having visited a lawyer five years ago to seek advice on what he'd termed as 'trying work conditions'.

As he struggled to keep up, Shindo felt a chill creep down his spine. Having only been transferred in the spring, Yanagi was still a newcomer to Station Q. And he was based in Criminal Investigations. Despite this, the level of detail was astounding. He was discussing, off the top of his head, the detailed affairs of officers from divisions other than his own. Right down to their age.

86

Shindo realised something.

He's no detective. The man's still Security.

The 'Berlin Wall' was a term used to describe a subtle transformation that had taken place in the Prefectural HQ. A crack had appeared in the once-inviolable ramparts that separated Security from the rest of the force, allowing a trickle of officers to flow into Criminal Investigations at a time when that department was under pressure because of an upturn in violent crime. The crack had, for the first time ever, created a link between two departments who each thought themselves number one. From an organisational standpoint, the event was no less significant than the fall of the Berlin Wall.

Yanagi was one of the officers who had been transferred out during what came to be known as the 'Berlin Departures'.

Prior to this he had worked under Shindo for two years as a member of the riot police, before being headhunted into Public Security, one of the department's core divisions. Shindo knew very little about the man's duties after that. They were both Security, but Shindo's time was spent in departments that were visible to the outside: working disaster response and the protection of key personnel. Public Security was different; their work, by definition, invisible. Even from a vantage point such as Shindo's, the division remained shrouded in fog.

It was, on occasion, unsettling.

There was one story he'd heard. Yanagi had picked up intel that the perpetrator of a mortar attack in Tokyo was lying low in the prefecture. He'd conducted a private investigation and after six long months had finally managed to pin down the man's location. He'd been ready to move in when an investigative team had swept in from the Public Security Bureau and robbed him of his quarry. The rumour was that Yanagi had set upon one of the investigators. The PSB had chosen to settle the matter amicably, yet it seemed likely that the incident had contributed to Yanagi's inclusion as a candidate for transfer.

Following his move out, Yanagi had spent his time working theft, moving from station to station in district. Yet Shindo had to wonder whether the work would be interesting enough for a man like Yanagi. Whether chasing down cases of larceny would truly excite him.

Shindo took a moment to collect his thoughts before he returned his focus to the phone. Yanagi's personal affairs were of little consequence. What mattered was that he would get the job done, and fast. *He serves a purpose*. That was how Shindo chose to justify his use of the man.

'Toshio Saga and Atsushi Mitsui. Got it. Do you know if either uses a word processor?'

'They both do.'

'Do you know the model?'

'Everything we use in the force is Brand K.'

'The question, then, is whether they have one at home.'

'I'll look into it.' There was a hint of excitement in his tone. Shindo saw the man's pallid features, reminiscent of a traditional Noh mask. Perhaps there was a grin on the man's thinly slanted lips.

He's enjoying this.

Shindo spoke faster. He asked Yanagi to conduct a background check on the *mama-san* and to get photos. After giving him a few more points to take note of, Shindo asked Yanagi if he had access to the roster for the night watch.

'Chief Sone is down for the thirtieth.'

Shindo put down the receiver.

It felt as though he were putting the lid on something dangerous.

I should at least pay Sone a visit, look him in the face. Yanagi had imme-diately known what Shindo was thinking. Not only that, he had already known the date that Sone – a man who wasn't even his boss – was scheduled for the night shift. Shindo felt a sudden pang of anxiety. *Yanagi's fangs, cutting through the informant, continuing until they reached Sone's guts.* The grotesque image manifested itself like a premonition.

Was it even possible to keep a man like Yanagi on a short leash?

It had started to rain. Shindo knew one person who would celebrate the fact. The thought was a pleasant distraction, but it wasn't enough to dismiss the voice from the phone still lingering in his ears.

4

The rain lasted until morning.

Shindo had put in an appearance at Internal Affairs but had returned to his apartment as soon as he'd updated Takegami on the situation. It was ten thirty when Yanagi's call came in, right on schedule.

'The fax machine is installed.'

'Let me send you what I have.'

Shindo faxed a copy of the letter. The response came in thirty minutes. The text was just as it had been in the original but the characters were now twice the size. Yanagi had typed the letter using a Brand K word processor, the one used by the force, and taken a copy in order to blow up the text. As it was still too early to rule out the possibility that the informant had used a word processor from the station, Shindo would take this to the crime lab for analysis.

He was getting to his feet when his eyes jumped back to the machine. The fax was in motion again. It droned and whirred, this time ejecting what seemed to be a photograph of a woman's face.

'I sent the original by registered mail,' Yanagi said when he answered the phone.

The woman in the photo – the *mama-san* – was standing with

her head poking out of the bar's front door, perhaps bidding a patron goodnight. The fax cast her features in shadow, making them appear harsh, but even so it was easy to see that she was strikingly attractive. Yet it was the face of the man on the other end of the phoneline that preoccupied Shindo's thoughts as he watched the paper feed through the machine. His speed off the blocks was incredible. He would have had to have headed into town late last night and used an infrared camera to get shots like these.

'Did you go inside?'

'No.'

'What about the background check?'

'I'll have it ready by tonight.'

Shindo thanked him and hung up. He left the building. Half of him regretted having involved Yanagi. He had other assets in the station, albeit none who had the man's investigative prowess. And he'd had the option of taking the case directly to the captain, or vice-captain, of the station. It was fairly standard, he knew, for an Internal Affairs inspector to take that route when investigating a case like this.

It'll be fine. Too late to do anything about it now.

After another lunch at the noodle bar Shindo bypassed his office to go directly to the crime lab on the fourth floor. Mizutani was looking bored, picking at a *bento*. Shindo asked if they could run a comparison against the retyped version of the letter. Mizutani told him it'd be a piece of cake. He put his chopsticks down and disappeared into the back, leaving behind his half-eaten lunch. Shindo had worried that the clarity of the faxed document would make a comparison difficult, but Mizutani had said nothing to suggest this would be an issue.

With no way of knowing how long the man would take, Shindo opted to wait for the results in Internal Affairs.

'Busy?' asked Katsumata, clearly probing.

Shindo muttered a non-committal response then returned to his work on drafting the commendations. With Katsumata there, he knew Takegami would not press him for an update.

Mizutani's 'piece of cake' turned out to take two hours.

'It's a completely different font.'

Shindo sighed. Still, he could at least now dismiss the possibility that the informant had used one of the force's machines. The troublemaker Toshio Saga, and the misfit Atsushi Mitsui – if he found that one of them had a different make of word processor at home . . .

The sound of a motorbike interrupted Shindo's line of thought. Takegami, already having put on his reading glasses, was reaching for the gloves in his drawer.

5

'They call her Ayumi in the bar, but her name is Yacko Kato.'

Yanagi reported in after Shindo returned home that night.

Yaeko Kato. Thirty-six. Twice divorced. Lives alone. Address: Room 806, Seventh Floor, Blue Heights Apartments, City P. Established Mumu three years ago after a period hopping from one bar to the next. Patron is a local loan shark who goes by the name of Oshima.

'Patron, huh? Did you find anything to link her to Sone?'

'Not yet.'

'Okay, I'll look into that. I want you to focus on Saga and Mitsui,' Shindo said, stressing the point again before he ended the call.

It seemed a good idea to have Yanagi work on the informant's identity, better than allowing him to investigate the relationship between Sone and Yaeko Kato. The man's arguments were airtight. As such, there would be no wiggle room should he conclude the claims in the letter to be true. That would be a hard pill to swallow. Sone was teetering on a cliff edge. He had been inspector longer than anyone else in the prefecture yet an anonymous tip-off was threatening to rob him of his final chance at promotion. Shindo did not wish the man's future as an officer to be decided by a single, indifferent report, one which he knew would not take the man's particular circumstances into account.

If it has to be done, I should be the one to do it.

Shindo turned to face the calendar on the wall. As he scanned the page, he realised it was still showing September. He got to his feet and tore it off, revealing a crisp, autumnal scene. The thirtieth. According to Yanagi, Sone was scheduled for the night watch in three days. *That's when I pay him a visit.* The decision was made.

'I'll know. I just need to look him in the face.'

The fax kicked into motion, as though responding to his words.

I hope you're taking your pills?

Fix the fucking calendar if you've got the time to worry about me. Shindo vented his irritation on the page showing September, crushing in his fist the relaxing image of an alpine pasture.

6

Yaeko Kato's looks surpassed all expectations.

It was the next day when Yanagi's parcel arrived containing the prints. The quality was incredible, considering he'd had to use an infrared camera.

Perfect.

Shindo headed out a little after midday, driving south down the national highway. Yamamoto, having contracted a throat infection, was forcing his listeners to endure an unpleasant stream of pop hits.

The traffic was, thankfully, light. And there was no need to look for the hotel; it slipped into view the moment he exited the highway. It was an odd structure, designed to look like a temple from Southeast Asia. Shindo swung around and into the parking area, crossing the sheets of multicoloured plastic which functioned as a barrier. He was familiar enough with this kind of place. As a young officer in district, he'd often made the rounds of these 'love hotels' when investigating cases of sexual misconduct.

He entered and called out as he approached the counter. After a short pause a stubbled face appeared, tilted sideways in the narrow aperture which connected the room on the other side. Shindo wasted no time in showing his ID.

'Don't worry, it's nothing to do with you,' he said. During

the course of living a normal life, of working for a wage, most people ended up with a blip or two that could be of interest to the force. That was why the first thing you did was make sure they felt at ease, get them to drop their guard.

Stubble proved no exception. He emerged from a side door, looking placid and half asleep. 'What do you want?'

Shindo decided to skip the introductions. He held out one of the photos of Yaeko Kato. 'Have you seen this woman here?'

Stubble nodded to confirm he had.

'Is she a regular?'

'I guess.'

'Okay. What about this man?' Shindo held out a photo of Sone, taken in profile. It was from his file in Internal Affairs, cropped neatly around the chin. He couldn't show the man's police uniform.

Stubble cocked his head to one side. 'Hard to say.' He didn't appear to be lying.

'She comes here with someone else?'

'I mean, there are a few of them . . .'

'More than one?'

'Sure, why not? She's a good-looking woman. This some kind of case?'

The man seemed to be waking up, which indicated to Shindo that this was a good time to stop asking questions. During any normal investigation he would have ordered a warrant, requested a list of car registration numbers alongside the log of calls from the room.

This time, his hands were tied.

Still, he'd made progress. Yaeko Kato frequented the hotel with various partners, yet Stubble had not recognised Sone's red face. If nothing turned up linking him to the bar, the letter could probably be dismissed as a case of unfounded slander.

Shindo allowed himself to relax during the drive back.

That leaves finding out who wrote the letter.

Shindo entered his apartment. There was a fax from Kanako asking him to call, followed by a single blank sheet. The signal that Yanagi wanted him to get in touch.

When the man answered, he said the words matter-of-factly: 'Sone has been frequenting Mumu.'

The thirtieth. Evening.

With a section chief behind the wheel, Shindo left to com-
mence the unscheduled inspection. Surprise checks such as these
were detested by the front-line officers in district and usually
referred to as 'raids'. Shindo had received the go-ahead after noti-
fying Takegami of his intention to inspect five stations to the
south. The chief had, of course, understood that Shindo's real
target was in Station Q.

Shaken by the motion of the car, Shindo's stomach was all
too tangible a presence. Despite his instructions to the contrary,
Yanagi had continued to look into the relationship between Sone
and Yaeko Kato. And the intel that Sone had been frequenting
Mumu was no doubt good, considering the source.

Shindo didn't like it.

I'll know when I see him.

With a headcount of more than 200 officers, Station Q was
one of the largest the prefecture had. The four-storey building
was old, with visible cracks, but a renovation last year and a
fresh lick of cream-coloured paint had allowed it to maintain
its status as a major hub in the south. It was seven thirty when
Shindo, wearing full uniform, stepped out of the car in front
of the station. A couple of young officers stood to attention,

giving sharp salutes as he walked through the glass entrance doors.

Table with local map. Riot shields at the ready, in case of forced entry.

Check.

Next was the ground floor. Shindo made the rounds of Transport, Administration and Accounting. Everything was in order. All the desks were tidy. His next stop was the armoury. Guns, bullets – everything was a match to the lists in inventory.

Shindo started to make his way up the stairs. He checked the now-empty divisions of the first, second and third floors. All the lights were off. All the windows were locked tight. He walked into Public Safety. Spotless. Apart from Sone's, the majority of desks were equipped with word processors. Shindo let his eyes linger on the logo: Brand K.

He took his time to make a thorough inspection of the detention facilities before finally returning to the ground floor. The officers on duty were there, standing in a line. Only those manning the radios were missing.

'Look smart!'

The order had come from the officer on watch, Yoshio Sone. His face was redder than ever, flushed with excitement and nerves. The checks began.

'Notebooks!'

The dozen or so officers present each held out their police notebooks. Once Shindo had inspected them, the order was given to put them away. Sone continued to bark orders: 'Rope!' 'Handcuffs!' 'Whistle!' 'Gun!'

Shindo found he could not look away as the man issued command after command, his voice almost screeching. This was the Sone he knew. He wasn't sure if it stemmed from sincerity or simple-mindedness but either way the man's sense of duty resembled that of an officer fresh out of police school. Even now, at fifty-five, he was almost hopelessly unchanged.

Sone has been frequenting Mumu.

Shindo couldn't picture him with Yaeko Kato. For this unremarkable middle-aged man who looked even now ready to collapse from stress to seduce an attractive *mama-san*, one who was well versed in the ways of the night. To gorge on her youthful body in a hotel. Try as he might, the image would not form in his mind. Even if Sone *had* been to Mumu, she wouldn't have paid him any attention, regardless of how hard he'd tried to win her over. Nothing could have happened between them.

Once the checks were complete, Shindo turned to face Sone.

'I'd like to take a look at the cars.'

It was the easiest way to get him alone. They left for the parking area behind the station, Sone with a bundle of keys in his hand. Shindo chose the car marked 'Q1'. Getting into the passenger seat, he asked Sone to start the engine.

'Front lights.'

'Yes, sir.' Sone's voice cracked.

'Back lights.'

'Sir.'

Sone shuffled his feet, looking awkward. Shindo twisted his neck to confirm the reflection of the red lights on the wall behind them.

Now.

He looked at Sone in profile. The man was covered in sweat.

'How are you doing?'

'Good. Thank you, sir.' He made no attempt to return Shindo's gaze. His eyes were fixed ahead, focused on the dark as he sat upright in his seat.

'I think we can dispense with the formalities. The *raid* is over.'

'Thank you, sir. If I may . . . I'm always impressed at how you conduct the inspections so thoroughly and with such precision.'

'Sone . . .'

Shindo felt his heart ache. It was true he was senior in terms of rank. Yet Sone had joined the force before him and had the edge when it came to age. And the two of them weren't strangers to each other. Outside work, in private like this, it was relatively common for the elder of two officers to talk as though they were addressing a junior. The force subscribed to a rigid hierarchy of rank but that didn't preclude the otherwise universal tradition of showing respect for your elders.

Yet Sone was different.

He seemed determined to give Shindo the respect appropriate for a superintendent. His tone remained formal and self-effacing throughout their conversation. This was what convinced Shindo of the man's innocence. He had not changed. His decency, his passion for the job, they were both as Shindo remembered.

Shindo pulled away from the station.

He imagined he could hear the sighs of relief but he knew the officers would be busy calling the nearby stations. *He's coming.* The next station in line would be scrambling to get everything in order.

It was close to eleven when he finally got back to the Prefectural HQ. A weak light seeped through the curtains of the room on the corner of the first floor of the north building.

As expected.

The officers from Administration were holed up in the cubbyhole that was Personnel. He'd been right – they'd already started work on the spring transfers. Shindo returned to Internal Affairs and sat at his desk to write up the evening's report.

There was a knock at the door.

'Do you have a moment?' Shinji Futawatari from Administration tipped his head into the room. 'How was the raid?'

'Good. Not that they're ever bad,' Shindo answered, choosing his words carefully.

Futawatari would have been there in Personnel. He would have come across after seeing the lights come on in Internal Affairs. Given the fact that it was after eleven, it was unlikely he'd come to chat. It was more likely that he'd been waiting for a chance to catch Shindo alone, when Takegami and Katsumata were out. That would be it.

People liked to refer to him as the 'ace'. He'd made superintendent three years ago, at the young age of forty. Such things had been known to happen, perhaps once every few generations, but Futawatari had another talent that separated him from the pack. In his case, the word 'ace' was also a reference to the trump card he held.

Personnel.

More than anything, it was the transfer he had masterminded two years previously that had propelled his name to the forefront.

Katsumata had gambled money during a game of mahjong with an acquaintance who owned a pachinko parlour. At the time, he'd been a division chief in Transport Guidance. One of his junior officers had been outraged and lodged an official complaint, which had led to Katsumata's eventual transfer.

The choice of destination had stunned the force.

Rather than face the scrutiny of Internal Affairs, Katsumata had been *transferred there*. It was inspired. The press, who had already caught wind of the scandal, had not known how to react. *They'd never move him there. Not if the rumours were true.* Futawatari had forced them to draw that conclusion.

Shirota doesn't have the gall to pull a stunt like that. I'm telling you, it was Futawatari. The whispers had spread like lightning through the force, the tone gradually shifting from one of shock to one of fear.

Even Shindo had to admit it was impressive. At the same time, he had to wonder whether such extreme measures had been necessary to safeguard the reputation of the force. There were scum wherever you went. Squeeze them out. That was surely the proper way to defend an organisation. However he looked at it, Shindo couldn't bring himself to fully agree with the man's way of thinking.

And yet, face to face with him now, this man who was seven years his junior, he couldn't help but feel intimidated.

It was second nature, after fifty, to think about how many years and how many posts you had left. While he couldn't quite match Futawatari's meteoric rise, Shindo was himself a career officer and one who had made superintendent at the age of forty-four. It had hurt to miss out on the promotion to district captain that spring but he still considered his stint in Internal Affairs to be temporary. It would last a year, at most, allowing him to recuperate. There was still time. He could still make director before his retirement.

Even so, another couple of years in some out-of-the-way post . . .

Shindo understood that the captain and the director of Administrative Affairs both held Futawatari in high regard. A single word from their 'ace' might be all it took to seal a man's fate, be the difference between making director and getting stuck at division chief.

'That reminds me,' Futawatari said, lowering his voice. 'Is something happening with Inspector Sone in Station Q?'

The words were like a slap in the face.

'No. I mean . . .' Shindo stumbled to find his response. 'We did have a letter, but I think it's one we can dismiss. He doesn't seem to be involved in anything untoward.'

'I see.'

Futawatari got smoothly to his feet. His footsteps grew distant and the room returned to silence. Shindo couldn't move from the couch.

Who told him?

He reviewed a selection of faces.

Takegami? Mizutani? No. *Yanagi?* Never. *Morishima from Forensics?* Not necessarily. Shindo had been to the Mutual Funds Association. And there was always the chance that Katsumata had somehow got wind of the letter. There was also the possibility that Futawatari had used some means of his own, although Shindo wouldn't usually expect a man who had spent his career in Administration to have too many 'assets' at his disposal. That said, people liked to back a winner and it wouldn't be long until Futawatari secured dominion over the Prefectural HQ. There would be plenty of people who wanted to win his favour. He wondered just how far the man's reach spread.

Whatever the source of the leak, the fact that Sone was now in Futawatari's sights meant that there were people outside Internal Affairs watching to see how Shindo handled the case. And work had already started on the transfers.

Shindo's stomach groaned, alerting him to an emotion that was a long way from anger.

8

'Toshio Saga doesn't own a word processor.'

Yanagi reported in a few days later. The troublemaker was off the list, then, leaving only the misfit Atsushi Mitsui. Shindo left Yanagi with instructions to continue looking into it but he felt more anxious than ever when he hung up.

How had Yanagi learned that Saga didn't own a word processor? Had he paid him a visit and found a chance moment to look around? That wouldn't be enough to support such a definitive conclusion. A frightening legal term came to mind. *Trespass.* Saga lived at home. Once he'd left for work, the house would be empty, apart from his bedridden mother. He *could* do it. He *would* do it. This was Yanagi.

Fuck.

Yanagi was still investigating Sone and Yaeko Kato. Shindo realised he wouldn't put it past the man to install a bug perhaps in the bar, or Yaeko's apartment – if it meant making progress. That would be a hassle, but Shindo had more to worry about. The case had caught Futawatari's attention. If Shindo lost control, if he let Yanagi go too far, he might end up paying for it with his career. He picked up the phone. *Don't do anything stupid.* He would spell it out for the man.

It was Yanagi's sister who answered. She told him her brother was out and that she didn't know where he had gone. Shindo was starting to panic.

Maybe I should go today.

His plan had been to visit Mumu in a few days but his current state of agitation told him he should perhaps bring the reconnaissance forwards. He hurried by taxi to City P and within thirty minutes was in the red-light district. He pushed his way past a collection of hawkers before he saw the bar's bright neon sign.

It was busy despite it being only eight in the evening. There were five booths inside, all of different sizes, and six seats along a counter. Three Southeast Asian women in skimpy, bikini-like clothing were draped over a group of sweaty men. Shindo guessed there might be more than alcohol on the menu.

'My my, a new face.'

A plumpish woman in a kimono appeared to greet him. She looked to be in her mid-forties and was oddly imposing. If he hadn't already seen the photos of Yaeko Kato, Shindo would have pegged her as the *mama-san*. She led him arm in arm to one of the seats at the counter and sat him down. They chatted for a while and he told her he was in town for three days to sell exercise equipment.

Yaeko Kato was in a bright-red dress. When she came into the room it was from under the *noren* which hung over the entrance to the kitchen; she was fiddling with her fringe.

'Welcome.'

She was just as beautiful in the flesh. Shindo suspected the bar had no need for the fawning girls, that men would flock in droves just to see her. The woman in the kimono gave a flick of her eye and Shindo was surrounded by dark, tanned skin. His ears were subjected to a stream of broken Japanese and hot air. The perfect time, perhaps. Yaeko was standing in front of him, mixing a glass of whisky on the rocks. Making it look as though he'd just remembered something, Shindo took out his mobile. He dialled the number of his apartment.

'Hey, it's me. Has Sone called yet?' Shindo kept an eye on Yaeko as he listened to the ringtone on the other side. 'You know who I mean. *So. Ne.*'

There was no reaction. Not even a twitch. The letter had been bogus. Sone had been a customer but Yaeko did not recognise his name. The only conclusion to draw was that Sone had used an assumed identity. It followed that he'd also hidden the fact that he was police. He hadn't played on his status as chief. Which made him the same as all the other customers — just another man here to see Yaeko. He couldn't have seduced her, not like that. His looks, too plain to attract a woman of her calibre, would end up becoming his saving grace.

Still, I'd bet the bastard gave it a good shot.

'Here. A token of our meeting.' Yaeko handed Shindo the glass and tapped her own against it.

'Thanks.'

Shindo put the whisky to his lips. His stomach lurched a little but he wanted, at least tonight, to drink a little in Sone's honour.

9

Sone turned out neither to have fallen for nor made a pass at
Yaeko Kato.

It was Monday morning, the last week of November, when
irrefutable proof of this arrived on the doorstep of Internal Affairs.
The intel came, surprisingly, in the form of a case report drafted
for the press by Media Relations.

'Shindo, you need to see this.' Division Chief Takegami, glasses
perched on his forehead, got to his feet and held out the document.

'Amazing.'

Late the previous night the Public Safety division in Station
Q had staged a raid on Mumu. The bar had been charged with
running a prostitution racket. For Shindo, the news was revelatory. Sone hadn't been trying to get Yaeko into bed. He'd
been trying to get her arrested. He'd concealed his name and
identity and made himself a customer as part of an undercover
investigation.

'Why all the fuss? It's not like this kind of thing never
happens.' Katsumata's head popped up at his side; he looked
unimpressed.

Shindo ignored him and walked up to Takegami. He suggested
they think about awarding Sone the Captain's Trophy. The district equivalent would have been given out the previous day.

It was perhaps too late but he wanted to try. The work on the executive transfers was almost finished. With a bit of luck, Sone might still get to hear his call from upstairs.

News continued to flow in. That afternoon Shindo received a call from Mizutani in the crime lab.

'We got the model of the word processor.' The man's usual tone was mixed with a hint of excitement, even pride. 'It's a Brand Z. Model 36. Only released a few months back.'

'I see. Good work.'

'It was blind luck more than anything else. One of the subsidiaries came up with this new typeface, just for the Model 36.'

'Typeface?'

'It's like a design, a blueprint for the characters. They worked out a way of keeping the *hiragana* nice and round, even when they're small. That's what gave it away.'

'This is good. I owe you a favour.'

Mizutani continued as though he hadn't heard the pleasantry. 'There's another thing you might find interesting. You remember the numbers six and nine had a gap between them?'

'Sure.'

'That means whoever typed the letter didn't know how to adjust the typeface so the numbers come out without the gap. Could be because it's a new model. Or it could be that whoever did this isn't very . . . well, very savvy with this kind of thing.' Mizutani was uncharacteristically talkative; it was clear he was in a celebratory mood.

Shindo told Takegami he was going out then set off for home.

He was in high spirits. The claims made against Sone had turned out to be false and he now had the model of the word processor. The case would be closed if the misfit Mitsui was discovered to own a Model 36. Now they had the make and model, they could investigate the shops that sold them. Shindo had to make double sure that Yanagi understood he wasn't to do anything reckless.

Time to rein him in.

A familiar voice began to relay the details of the raid on Mumu. Yamamoto played up the sense of sleazy indignation as he outlined how the five women who worked at the bar had been robbed of their passports, how they'd been forced to live cramped together in a small tatami room. He mentioned Yaeko Kato but went on to name the ringleader as Sasaki, a woman of forty-six.

Huh.

The plumpish woman in the kimono came to Shindo's mind. It was obvious, in retrospect. Sasaki had been manipulating Yaeko from the shadows. She was the *mama-san*.

'But that's . . .'

The *mama-san*. Shindo's mind lurched. It would be only natural, on seeing Sasaki for the first time, to conclude that she was the proprietress. Yet one man had reached a different conclusion.

Shindo felt a sudden dizziness, followed by the sensation of everything falling neatly into place. The misfit was gone. In his place stood the informant, the man who had set his sights on Sone. Shindo parked his car and made his way slowly up the stairs. His stomach convulsed under the full weight of his fury.

He ran a blank sheet through the fax.

10

Shindo met Yanagi at Leisure Land in City Y, on the border of the prefecture. He'd opted to do it on a Sunday. The man appeared, bang on schedule at two o'clock in front of the big wheel. He was wearing a jacket, his pallid features seeming to float amidst the throngs of families. Shindo was wrapped in a warm coat and sitting on a bench. They both resembled tired parents whose weekends had been eaten up by family outings. Yanagi set himself down on the same bench, leaving space for one person between them.

'It was you,' Shindo said, keeping his gaze forwards.

'Sorry?' Yanagi, too, was looking ahead.

'You were the one who tried to frame Sone.'

'Me?'

'I can see it, you know. The scenario you came up with, acted out. You figured I'd come to you if something came up regarding Station Q. Everything was going to plan.'

'. . .'

'I should have realised that something was off. You knew too much from the start. All that detail on Saga and Mitsui. You even knew the day Sone was scheduled for night watch.' In the periphery of his vision, Shindo thought he caught the Noh mask smirk. 'Something amusing?'

'. . .'

'You told me on the phone that you hadn't been inside the bar, that time you took the photos of Yaeko Kato.'

'Sure.'

'What made you think Yaeko was the *mama-san*? I seem to remember it wasn't until the next day that you started looking into her background.'

'I'd been there before.'

Shindo turned to face him. 'You didn't tell me that.'

'I didn't think I needed to.'

Shindo looked straight ahead again. 'Let me be specific. You found out that Atsushi Mitsui owned a Brand Z, Model 36 word processor. You picked one up for yourself and used it to type out the letter. I asked you to look into the case, as expected, and you proceeded to give me one revelatory detail after another. It was after we learned the model of the word processor, right? That was when you'd planned to reveal that Mitsui had one.'

'Why would I do that? I don't have anything against Sone or Mitsui.'

Shindo looked up at the sky as he answered. 'My guess is . . . because you wanted to return to Public Security.'

This time the Noh mask broke into an open smile.

'You were transferred out. You lost your connections with the executive. That's why you cooked up this whole fiasco. To impress me with your talents. On the assumption that I'd be heading back there myself.'

Yanagi got to his feet and fixed Shindo with a cold stare. 'Sir, let me be perfectly clear. I've never considered you a superior.'

11

The year drew to a close.

Shindo had cultivated a new asset in Station Q. He'd left the man, Takeshi Sato, with standing instructions to investigate the situation between Yanagi and Mitsui. *They should both have a Model 36. Take your time, be thorough.* Despite his words, the passing of time had left Shindo feeling increasingly agitated. Yanagi was dangerous. And Shindo could not accept the way he'd tried to use Sone, a man already standing on a cliff edge, as leverage in his plan. He needed definitive evidence to relieve the man of his badge, and soon.

He was the misfit.

The new year came amidst an atmosphere of frustration. Kanako had come home for the end of December but returned to Tokyo on New Year's Eve, claiming their daughter had cram sessions during the first few days of the year. Was that really the way to go about achieving your dreams? Shindo just didn't get it.

He was sorting through their New Year cards when the fax began to buzz. He ignored it, assuming it to be Kanako's usual update, only to discover an hour later that it had ejected a blank sheet. He rushed to dial Sato's number. It was 3 January. Sato had taken advantage of the holidays to get what he needed. That had to be it.

'Did you get something?'

'Sir, it seems neither Yanagi nor Mitsui owns a Brand Z.'

'Seems?'

'Not that I could see, at least.'

Shindo ended the call. This was, he supposed, the limit of what they could realistically do. If the machines were hidden, it would be next to impossible to find them. There was also the chance that they had been sent for scrap. Only when you were writing your own scenario, as Yanagi had, was it possible to categorically state that someone *had* or *did not have* something in their possession.

Except that . . .

The same logic didn't apply in the case of Mitsui. The latter would have no knowledge of the fact that he'd been set up. He would have no reason to hide anything. Which meant Sato should have found something when he'd searched the man's home.

He doesn't have one?

It didn't make sense. Yanagi's plan would fall apart if Mitsui wasn't in possession of a Model 36. He had to have one for the conclusion to play out.

Which means . . .?

Shindo couldn't sleep that night. It was almost sunrise when the first ripples of an idea disturbed the quiet of his mind. These grew into tall, overpowering waves, which eventually drove him from his bed. A scene from his raid on Station Q was stuck on repeat, cast in a blinding light. Accompanying this was the beating pulse of Mizutani's voice. Shindo was almost in despair by the time the sun finally came up.

He'd realised the truth.

12

Shindo made his move during the first few weeks of the year.

It was night-time. He pushed the buzzer on the door of the police-issued apartment. The man's wife answered without make-up, her hair pulled up into a bun. Looking a little startled, she scampered back indoors when Shindo introduced himself. He saw her lugging a cardboard box from one room to another. Judging by the markings, it contained components for an indicator light. A nearby factory had started subcontracting for a bike manufacturer and a number of the residents in the nearby apartments had opted to take up a lucrative sideline in assembling parts. Her husband appeared shortly, looking worried. Following his invitation, Shindo entered the apartment.

He took a sheet of paper from his shirt pocket and slid it across the tatami so it rested in front of the man's knees.

'I believe this is yours.'

> *Division Chief of Public Safety, Station Q*
> *Seeing Proprietress of Mumu*
> *Hotel 6 9*

Shindo watched Kazuo Sone's red face turn crimson. It was difficult to look him in the eye.

He'd been behind it all. He'd typed the letter, framing himself and pushing Internal Affairs to launch an investigation. He'd cast a spotlight on his disgrace only to reveal a twist at the end, in his unmasking of the prostitution racket.

He had thought: *I'll be promoted. I'll make damn sure of it.*

His desperation must have been overwhelming. Somewhere along the line it had taken the shape of this all-or-nothing gamble.

Seventeen years had been too much.

Back when Shindo had conducted his raid on Station Q, Sone's had been the only desk not to have a word processor. Mizutani had suspected the letter to be the work of someone who lacked experience with such machines. If Shindo had put the two facts together, they would have led him to Sone.

But he hadn't. He couldn't have.

The shame burned.

He'd been convinced that the claims were fabricated. That was why he'd cast his suspicion on Yanagi. He'd made it that far. Why, then, had he not seen the possibility that the very same idea might arise in the mind of the prefecture's longest-serving inspector?

Shindo was one of those who had made superintendent and left Sone behind. He'd never spared a thought for the man. His focus had always been on chasing those still battling ahead of him. That was why he'd been unable to see it, the heartbreakingly flawed scheme of this man who'd contrived to betray his own decency.

Sone was trembling. From his hands and knees, all the way to the back of his bowed-down head, the man's body depressingly betrayed his emotions. A uniform, freshly starched, hung on the lintel of the wall. There was a dull glint on the badge that denoted his rank as inspector. There was a water stain on the wardrobe door. Open that, and it would all be over.

The Model 36.

'Sone.'

'Sir, this isn't . . .' He collapsed forwards, his shaking fingers threading protectively around the letter. He buried his head in the tatami. 'Sir, this isn't what you . . .'

His voice seemed to well up from the ground.

Unheeded by the heavens for seventeen years, it was the cry of the earth.

13

The details of transfers for officers ranked inspector and above were released two weeks later.

Shindo was in Internal Affairs when he picked up a copy of the document. He flicked to the last page. It was the first time he'd started with a name other than his own. *Promotions: Superintendent.* There were seven names on the page. Kazuo Sone wasn't among them.

Guess it wasn't enough.

Shindo took a moment to compose himself then turned back to the front. *What?* He flicked to the next page, then the next, and again. His hands were shaking. It wasn't there. His name was nowhere to be seen.

One more year.

His stomach growled at the idea.

'Looks like we'll be together a bit longer,' Katsumata said, not smiling. He was still paying the price for his game of mahjong. No doubt having expected as much, he didn't seem particularly dejected.

Shindo gave notice that he was leaving early then went out into the corridor. His gut was burning with indignation. The door to Administration was open. Futawatari was sitting at his desk at the back of the room. He gave a brief tip of his head to acknowledge Shindo's presence.

Futawatari.

Shindo was hit by a realisation.

Sone would have sent a copy of his letter to Administration. Maybe not even a copy. It was possible Administration had been his primary target. Send a single letter to Internal Affairs and you risked Administration – the section in charge of transfers – never finding out. That would have reduced the impact of Sone's unveiling of the prostitution racket. The pieces were falling into place. The *copy* had been sent to Internal Affairs, and only to raise the stakes.

Futawatari had, of course, seen through the man's subterfuge. He'd seen the truth behind the one-man show. And he'd known that Shindo had allowed it to go unpunished.

His chance of making director felt further away than ever. He knew he hadn't joined the force with the express purpose of making it to the top. And he realised it was his own core beliefs that had compelled him to turn a blind eye to Sone's actions.

And yet.

He suspected it would stay with him until the day he retired. The grudge he now held against the decent, hard-working, red-faced inspector.

It was this part of himself which became the final target of his anger.

With no destination in mind, Shindo pulled out of the parking area. He saw Yanagi's Noh mask. He saw Kanako and Akiko, standing together, the former frowning and anxious, the latter deep in concentration. They seemed far away. Out of reach.

Yamamoto was the only one who remained close by, declaring, with unwavering confidence, that they would see snow by evening.

Shindo hammered his fist into the radio then reached instinctively for his gut.

Half gone and you still hurt like fucking hell.

A motorbike shot down the prefectural highway. Shindo knew, without checking the time, that it was three in the afternoon.

BLACK LINES

'Officer Hirano hasn't come in?'

Prefecture D Police Headquarters, Administration. Section Chief Tomoko Nanao, in charge of the female officers in the prefecture, found herself parroting the words.

'That's right. Maybe the fame's gone to her head?'

The glum voice belonged to Division Chief Mitsuo Morishima of Forensics. He was claiming that Sergeant Hirano, part of the Mobile Forensics team, had not shown up at work. That they'd heard nothing all morning. Tomoko glanced at the clock on the wall.

Already ten thirty.

'Maybe she's ill? Did you get in touch with the dorm?'

'I did. The caretaker said she left as usual this morning. In her car, at seven thirty.'

'Okay. Leave it to me.'

'Thanks, Sniffer.'

Fifteen years ago, Tomoko had also worked at Mobile Forensics. Her heightened sense of smell had led to her nickname of 'Sniffer', a reference to the abilities of the police dogs. Morishima, her team leader at the time, had coined it himself. Now she was forty-two and he was the last member of the force to persist in using it.

She hung up the phone, finding the fact a little hard to process. *Mizuho Hirano*.

At twenty-two, she was in her fifth year as police sergeant. She was pretty, with the kind of dainty features that were always in vogue. At the same time, her brownish hair and eyes combined with a generally light complexion to form an impression that was somewhat lacking in impact. This belied a strong will, however, and the girl had worked tirelessly to achieve her dream of becoming an officer of the law. She was conscientious and had a genuine wish to help. Questions of gender aside, she was exactly the type of officer the force needed.

It was hard to imagine someone like her taking a day off without notice. She valued her work and had become an integral part of her team. More to the point, today should have been her special day. Morishima had alluded to it on the phone: the morning newspapers were all running articles on her latest achievement.

'Officer Nanao. Do you have a moment?'

The voice came from the desk behind her. Inspector Futawatari was skimming one of the articles covering the previous day's events. He had no doubt overheard her conversation with Morishima. She'd noticed when the tang of his hair wax had returned, but had decided to ignore him, still irked at his earlier rejection of her draft plans to reassign the female officers in the prefecture.

She guessed she no longer had that luxury.

One of the morning papers lay open on his desk. A collection of upbeat headlines jumped up from the middle section of the local pages.

Female Officer's Triumph. Spitting Image. Bag-snatcher Arrested.

Tomoko already knew the gist of the article.

A seventy-year-old woman had her bag snatched yesterday on the pavement outside Train Station M. Police Sergeant Mizuho Hirano arrived to question her and drew a likeness of her assailant. Police used the drawing in their investigation. Upon seeing it, a local store owner proclaimed it the spitting image of a man he knew. The arrest of the twenty-year-old male, living behind the station, was made within the hour.

The coverage was impressive, even considering the lack of newsworthy events the previous day, and especially so in light of the favourable tone. The likeness Mizuho had drawn was reproduced next to a mugshot of the assailant, as though to emphasise its incredible accuracy. A small photo of Mizuho had been included at the bottom, the one Morishima had attached to the drawing and the other documents he'd handed to the press during the previous day's briefing at the Press Club.

That day, Tomoko had rushed over to Forensics during her lunch break. When she'd congratulated Mizuho, the girl had responded with all the bubbly giddiness of a girl in high school. Tomoko had even promised to take her out for *anmitsu*, a celebratory dessert, over the weekend. What reason could Mizuho possibly have for not coming in?

Futawatari raised his eyes from the article.

'Has anything like this happened before?'

'No, never. She's not the type to take time off without letting her team know.'

'Okay. So what does this mean?' Futawatari looked straight at her. With his thin profile silhouetted against the light of the window, all Tomoko could see was the keen glint in his eyes.

'It's hard to say, sir.'

Even as she spoke, a string of unpleasant words unfolded in her mind. *Trouble. Accident. Crime.* Futawatari was silent, sitting with his arms folded. His eyes were skimming back over the article. It was possible he feared the same thing.

There was one particular detail which had caught her attention when she'd read one of the articles earlier that day. *The assailant had previously led a biker gang.* She'd told herself it would be fine. That there wasn't a gang out there with the gall to launch a direct attack on the police. And yet, she knew that certain types of scum refused to consider women real officers of the law. There was also the fact that the press had distributed tens of thousands of copies of their articles, each mentioning that Mizuho's drawing had been directly responsible for the arrest and each printing her name and photograph.

Whatever the cause of her absence, the fact remained that Mizuho had not come in on what would be a special day for her. Tomoko felt increasingly concerned that something had happened.

'I'll go and check at the dorm.'

'Leave me the model and registration of her car before you go.'

Tomoko grimaced at the request. Futawatari was planning to send a bulletin to the other stations. Maybe it was the right move. It was important to cover all bases. Tomoko handed him the details on a memo then hurried out.

He called after her.

'Phone if you find out anything.'

He looked uneasy. Tomoko took this as confirmation that he, too, was considering a number of unwelcome outcomes. She knew that the high-flying superintendent, who was two years her senior and the implicit authority behind all things related to personnel, would be unlikely to do anything that would draw attention to himself. Yet she also knew that his delicate appearance belied an incredible tenacity, that he was one of the most committed individuals in the force when it came to averting a crisis.

In the locker room Tomoko changed back into her civilian clothes. There was the possibility of more legwork after the dorm and her uniform would only slow her down. A middle-aged woman gazed back from the small mirror on the inside of the locker door. She didn't even flinch. There was still beauty there, she thought, in the narrow eyes, in the curved line of her mouth. The mirror had been with her since she was eighteen. It had witnessed her tears, her laughter, everything there was to see. She could face it with confidence, knowing she needn't conceal the sagging of her skin or the wrinkles forming around her eyes.

Tomoko was the only female officer in the Prefectural HQ who was ranked inspector. She was elder sister and mother to forty-eight women, a number that was greater than the total headcount of some of the smaller stations in district.

She didn't have time for make-up.

She left the main building and set off quickly towards the parking area. *She'll be fine. It'll turn out to be nothing.* This was her habit. Her first step was always to banish any fears or worries that were festering inside her. For twenty-five years she'd steeped herself in a world that was dominated by men. She knew only too well that fragility was the single greatest threat you could face as a female officer.

2

Tomoko kept her foot on the accelerator and in fifteen minutes was pulling on the handbrake in the parking area of the female officers' dorm.

Designed with the primary consideration of blending in with its surroundings, the building looked like any other block of apartments. Like their male counterparts, the prefecture's female officers were required to spend five years in a dorm after their graduation from police school. Men were off limits. Curfew was at ten. The force was perhaps famous for enforcing draconian policies such as these, but Welfare was happy enough to relinquish its control should a decent suitor be found – as had been the case for Tomoko – during this period.

The dorm's caretaker, Toshie Hatsuda, bustled out the moment Tomoko called from the entranceway.

'Nanao, have you heard anything from Mizuho?'

'Not yet.'

'I see. Oh . . . what should we do?'

If memory served, Toshie was around ten years Tomoko's senior, which would put her in her mid-fifties. She had no children. Her husband, an officer from Mobile Investigations, had died in the line of duty, stabbed while investigating a break-in during the summer twelve years ago. Toshie had since, by way of an introduction from Administration, devoted herself to her role as caretaker of the female officers' dorm.

It was this history which caused Tomoko's heart to ache every time she set eyes on the woman. She, too, had been married to an officer. Despite a bright future in Security, he had passed away three years earlier. He hadn't died in the line of duty, not specifically. But Tomoko could not help wondering, every now and then, whether he hadn't suffered something close to *karoshi*, the now infamous death from overwork.

Toshie led her to the canteen, where vegetables for the evening meal were already laid out in neat groups on the tables.

'She left without breakfast this morning.'

'Sorry, I'm not hungry,' Mizuho had said before she left. That had been at seven thirty. It was the time she usually left for work. She'd been wearing a cream dress. It was one of a few she generally wore for her commute. She'd had a little make-up on, but nothing drastic. The only thing that was slightly different, according to Toshie, was that she'd seemed a little down.

'How about the night before?'

'She was late back. I mean, she gets these early and late calls for work, so that's not necessarily anything to . . .'

Tomoko nodded.

Whenever a serious crime took place within the prefecture, Mobile Forensics would be called to the scene. Their job was to collect footprints, fingerprints and all other trace forms of evidence. Mizuho would join her team in the mini-van as it raced to its destination. Drawing likenesses was only a side job.

Toshie went on to say that Mizuho had not arrived back until after the ten o'clock curfew. She'd called into the caretaker's office from the corridor, apologised for being late and said goodnight. She'd been out of sight by the time Toshie had emerged from the room; she'd heard only the sound of her footsteps in the stairwell. They'd seemed to lack their usual vitality, and Toshie remembered thinking that Mizuho must be tired.

It didn't fit.

Toshie was claiming that Mizuho had been out of sorts, but that was strange. Mizuho had been celebrating her triumph with a childlike glee during lunch that day. Tomoko had witnessed the girl's wide-eyed joy in person. Had something happened after that? Something to cut short her celebratory mood prior to her return to the dorm at ten? Something to nullify her excitement? An overwhelming shock of some kind?

A man?

It was the first thing to come to mind.

'Do you know if she's seeing anyone?'

'Seeing anyone? Oh, I don't think so. She's as straight-laced as they come. No, I'm pretty sure she isn't.'

Tomoko recoiled at the defensive tone. She noted a sense of envy, too, for Toshie's closeness to Mizuho. While Tomoko knew that she did not doubt the girl's virtue either, Toshie's display of motherly affection forced her to accept that she was now acting in her capacity as a managing officer. Perhaps that had been the woman's intention. *We've both lost husbands in the force. But you've still got your son. Let me at least have the girls.* This plea was something that was always there in her eyes.

The grandfather clock in the canteen began to chime.

Eleven thirty.

Four hours had passed since Mizuho had left the dorm. Given the time and the fact that they'd yet to hear anything, it seemed safe to dismiss the idea of a traffic accident. And, while she couldn't yet dismiss the possibility of a crime having taken place, Tomoko's conversation with Toshie had served to greatly alleviate her fears regarding the bike gang. If Mizuho had been out of sorts since the previous night, it seemed likely that her going missing was related to whatever it was that had altered her mood.

Missing.

The word caught Tomoko off guard. Missing, not absent. Perhaps it was appropriate. Who was to say it wouldn't continue beyond today? That the situation would change tomorrow, or the day after? Surely she had to consider the possibility.

Female officer. Location unknown.

Tomoko got to her feet.

'Can I see her room?'

Toshie nodded and began to walk towards her office. She stopped suddenly, as if she'd just remembered something. She riffled through her apron and pulled out a key with a sticker marked 'Room 6'.

'You've been inside?'

'Yes. I thought she might have left a note, but I didn't see anything.'

A note, maybe on her desk, explaining the absence.

Tomoko had entertained that hope, too, and was discouraged to learn that no such thing existed. Still, there might be other clues. She should at least check.

She made for the stairs; she knew her way around. She made sure to be present whenever someone was moving in or out and she made frequent rounds to lend an ear to the concerns of the younger officers. Still, she was never sure whether it made a difference. Mizuho had disappeared without so much as a word. And Tomoko, for her part, was unable to come up with a single theory as to why.

First floor. Room six.

There were two names on the door: Mizuho Hirano and Junko Hayashi. Tomoko turned the key. The air shifted when she opened the door, causing something to tickle her nose.

Perfume?

Anyone else might have missed it. The scent was faint but clearly identifiable. Tomoko had a natural aversion to the stuff. The unexpected olfactory greeting caused her to hesitate. Not once had she detected even a whiff of perfume on either Mizuho or her roommate – not on them, and certainly not in their room.

Mizuho's bedroom was located to the right of a common space which contained the bath, toilet and other facilities. The door was unlocked. Tomoko's heart pounded as she pushed it open. The scent grew stronger. It was Mizuho's.

The small bottle sat on what looked like a kid's dresser. *Chanel No. 19.* Not one to use perfume herself, Tomoko had only a limited knowledge of such things. Yet even she knew that this particular brand was one men liked to give as a present to women.

A man, then.

Tomoko let out a deep sigh before scanning the remainder of the room in an attempt to calm herself down. A collection of faces decorated one of the walls. The drawings were of actors, celebrities, news anchors, comedians and various other TV personalities and were arranged in neat rows. Tomoko had had to catch her breath the first time she'd set eyes on the collection. Mizuho had been working hard. Really hard.

A likeness was a drawing of a suspect based on information provided by victims and witnesses to a crime. Deemed to be greater in accuracy than the photo composites used before them, they had been fully integrated into the investigative toolset of every station in the country. Mizuho was the third female officer in the prefecture to have taken on the role of drawing them. Seeing in her greater potential than she saw in her predecessors, Forensics had taken an active role in developing her abilities. They had placed her under the tutelage of a well-known painter and paid for her to attend the municipal art school twice a week.

Their investment had paid off.

The likeness she had drawn of the gang leader had proved astoundingly accurate. She had justified the expectations of her department and raised her standing in the force as a whole. Tomoko had been proud. An officer under her guard had committed herself to working towards a goal and been rewarded for her effort.

And yet . . .

The pictures on the wall. The little bottle on the dresser. Which, Tomoko wondered, was the better reflection of what Mizuho wanted now?

Tomoko caught Toshie on her way out. 'Was she wearing perfume when she left?'

'Perfume? Not that I noticed. She doesn't really like that sort of thing, you know,' Toshie said, nudging her head out of her room, defensive again, smelling ever so slightly of perfume herself.

Tomoko set off for the Prefectural HQ.

Junko would be at her desk in Traffic Planning. As Mizuho's roommate, she would have more information. About the perfume. And about the man.

Wait.

A short pause at the lights was enough for Tomoko to find a question. Mizuho had left in her usual commuting attire. She'd had some make-up on, but nothing out of the ordinary. Why, then, bother with perfume? Mizuho was of course smart enough not to wear anything that would grab attention even if she *had* been on her way to meet someone. And if the relationship was sufficiently advanced, there would be no need to dress up anyway.

The lights turned green.

Tomoko pressed down on the accelerator. It was already after twelve. The movement of the clock marked the gradual transition of Mizuho's status from *absent* to *missing*.

3

Junko Hayashi seemed a little taken aback to see Tomoko show up in her everyday clothes.

Tomoko led her away from her desk and sat her down on a bench in the courtyard. Once they were sitting next to each other, Tomoko reclaimed the advantage in height. As they both met the height restrictions set out for female officers, what this meant was that Junko had remarkably long legs. She sat with her knees together, her double-lidded eyes – the kind men found hopelessly attractive – looking disoriented at being called out so abruptly. She appeared not to have known about Mizuho's absence.

'But, that's . . . I mean, she was dressed to come in.'

'I know. Did you leave with her?'

'No. I left before her.'

'Had she been acting strangely?'

'Strangely? I don't think so. No different to usual.'

'How about last night?'

'Let's see. I had an early night. Didn't hear her get back, actually. I was out like a light, don't think I heard a thing.'

Junko was the type who, in any lengthy conversation, tended to lose sight of the fact that she was an officer of the law. Tomoko was frustrated by the lack of new information but it wasn't the only reason she felt like stamping her foot. She had been a teacher at police school at the time of Junko's graduation.

You just make sure you don't end up being exploited for your looks.

Seeing the potential for this in her, Tomoko had given the warning on the day of her graduation. The girl was, as feared, already becoming a trophy-like figure in Traffic Planning. She was a hit with the senior officers. *Fetching tea. Running errands. Playing hostess at drinks parties.* She had a penchant for flaunting her brilliant white teeth, even at work, appearing to completely forget the fact that she was in uniform.

It was, Tomoko reasoned, one way of getting on. The force was dominated by men, so it was probably the path of least resistance. And yet she knew that every one of her officers had, at some point, made the conscious decision to become an officer of the law. She didn't ask that they put themselves in direct competition with the male officers but she did hope that they at least carve a niche for themselves, something they could be proud of, however modest. It was the only way to forge a path for their successors and the only way to silence those in the force who argued for their expulsion.

Catching sight of a female guidance officer from Juvenile Crime, Junko moved her hand in a small wave next to her abdomen. *Look who's got me.* Perhaps she'd pulled a face to signal something like that, too.

Tomoko shook off her disappointment and returned to the subject at hand. 'Mizuho owns a bottle of Chanel.'

'Really?'

Junko's expression showed that she was nervous. And, if she was getting apprehensive, that probably meant she knew something. Tomoko realised it would be hard to get anything out of her if she let her slip into a *girls protect girls* mindset. She eased in closer, up to the point where she was almost choking on the smell of shampoo.

'Look, I'm trying to find her but I need something I can work with. Do you understand?'

'Sure.'

'Tell me, then, did she buy the perfume? Or did someone give it to her?'

'She said it was a present.'

'Do you know who from? Don't worry, I can keep a secret. I just need to know.'

Junko sighed as though to say, *Fine*, if she had no choice. 'She told me it was one of the reporters.'

'What?' Tomoko felt suddenly dizzy. A reporter mixing with a female officer? It was the type of relationship the force hated and feared the most. She lowered her voice to a whisper. 'Are they seeing each other?'

'No. I mean, it's not like that. It's more like he's her stalker.'

Junko began to ramble, her focus wandering from one subject to the next, but Tomoko managed to catch most of the salient points.

The reporter had developed a crush on Mizuho. One night, about a month back, he'd waited for her in the dorm's parking area. When Mizuho had returned from work he'd handed her the perfume, claiming it to be a souvenir from a foreign business trip. Mizuho had, of course, refused to take it, but he'd pressed it into her hands and walked away. For a long time Mizuho had fretted over what to do. *What do you think? Should I tell him to take it back?* She had, it seemed, solicited Junko's advice on several occasions.

'What's his name?' Tomoko asked, sighing again.

'She told me she doesn't know it.'

Mizuho, it seemed, knew neither the man's name nor which

paper he worked for. She knew his face, but only because they kept ending up at the same crime scenes. That, at least, was what she'd told Junko.

'She might have been hiding some of the truth. She liked to complain about him but she looked kind of happy at the same time.'

There was something in her eyes when she said this, some kind of spite or whimsy. Tomoko realised Junko would want to use the bathroom and fix her make-up. She released the girl ten minutes before lunchtime was over then began to make her way back to the main building.

Perfume. Reporter. Unscheduled absence.

She knew they were connected somehow, yet the pieces refused to come together. It had all happened too quickly. Only a month had passed since the reporter gave Mizuho the perfume. And even supposing their relationship *had* blossomed since then, it was still no reason for her to run away. The force might view their kind of relationship as taboo but society as a whole had no issues with a policewoman seeing a reporter. All she had to do to fix the problem was leave the force. Still, Tomoko understood that love could be a problem in itself. It had been known, in the past, to cause trouble on a scale that was hard to imagine.

At this stage, Tomoko had more or less dismissed the idea of a crime having occurred. A female officer, missing. She understood the severity of the situation, yet it was becoming increasingly difficult to ignore her feelings of disappointment. Whatever her reasons, it seemed more and more likely that Mizuho had decided to disappear. What, given that, was the point in hunting her down and dragging her back?

In the locker room Tomoko changed back into her uniform. It was easy to recall the elation she'd felt the first time she'd threaded her arms through the sleeves of her shirt. The sense of pride had not faded at all. Yet there'd been a time when even she had questioned herself. She still did, probably, just under the surface. She'd worried that the uniform was ungainly. That it was nothing special. That, just maybe, she'd been destined for other things. Perhaps Mizuho had simply made the decision to move on.

Tomoko left the room.

The ring on her left hand reminded her of her husband. She chided herself for thinking of him now, for wanting yet again to seek his advice, but she could not rid herself of the desire to convey her sense of helplessness to the silver object.

4

Futawatari was out.

Tomoko felt partly relieved, having not been sure whether she should report what she'd learned about the perfume and the reporter. At the same time, she'd been hoping to ask for advice on how to proceed. While she wasn't sure how far she could trust him, she knew he was the only senior officer in Administration with whom she felt safe discussing the matter.

The couch in front of the chief's desk was overflowing with high-level officers from the various divisions of Administrative Affairs, each bearing a stack of papers. The daily pilgrimage to Akama's office was, it seemed, already underway.

Hajime Akama.

The man had been appointed as successor to Director Oguro, the ever formidable and authoritarian leader of Administrative Affairs, following the latter's transfer to the Regional Police Bureau in the spring. Those who had suffered under his rule had breathed a sigh of relief to see his gentle-looking replacement. Their celebrations had, of course, been short-lived. Akama turned out to have an obsession for statistics. He demanded reports on everything, spreading his focus across the whole department and pursuing even the tiniest of details. With a compulsion that bordered on the pathological, he called for data on everything from the number of batons being used in the substations to the number of trees the force had planted around the police apartments.

The result was a threefold increase in the workload.

Everyone had to have the answer to hand, backed up by the relevant data, whatever the NPA or the captain should ask. Akama's goal, no doubt, was to carve himself a role as the prefecture's most trusted functionary.

Tomoko picked up the phone, keeping an eye on the excited procession of chiefs filing in and out of the man's office. It was one in the afternoon, already long past the time she could justifiably delay informing Mizuho's parents of the fact that their daughter was missing.

She was trying to work out how to broach the subject when Mizuho's mother answered and she found out there was no need.

Morishima had already called.

'I'm so sorry. This must be causing you so much trouble.'

The woman would have been sick with worry, yet despite this her tone was primarily one of apology. *Married to the force.* That was perhaps how Mizuho's parents, both farmers, had decided to rationalise their only daughter leaving home. Tomoko realised she had, until this point, been holding on to the hope that Mizuho would be there, that everything might be resolved without further incident. But Mizuho had not gone home. Far from it: she hadn't even called. Her mother's voice was almost inaudible when she confessed that she couldn't think of a single reason why Mizuho would want to run away.

Shirota approached the moment Tomoko ended the call.

'Any progress?'

'Not yet,' Tomoko said, not wanting to give any details.

She knew Shirota would pass anything she said on to Akama, who, aside from his obsession with detail, was also one of the force's principal advocates for the total exclusion of women. Shirota, too, was acting in far too blasé a manner. Was it so trivial for a female officer to go missing? Was he simply clinging to the idea that, despite the time that had passed, this was simply a case of unreported absence? *She's Forensics. Criminal Investigations should look after their own.* Maybe that was how he saw it.

'Do you know where Futawatari went?'

'He said he was going to the bank.'

The bank. That meant he had probably gone to check the details of Mizuho's account. If she'd taken out any substantial sums of money, that would support the theory that she'd run away of her own accord.

Once free of Shirota, Tomoko took the chance to leave the office. She wanted to catch up with Morishima before Futawatari returned.

The fourth floor was host to the various divisions of Criminal Investigations and as such was often given a wide berth by the officers of Administrative Affairs. For Tomoko, however, Forensics felt like a second home. There was nothing here that intimidated her.

She saw Morishima's bulldog-like features behind his desk. He was discussing something with Yuasa, who led the Mobile Forensics team, but raised his hand in greeting when he saw her come in.

'Any luck at the dorm?'

The three reconvened on a couch behind a partition that closed off an area from the rest of the room. Tomoko's nose bristled at the mix of Morishima's pomade and Yuasa's hair oil. It was also evident that neither feared the effects of smoking on their mortality.

Tomoko summarised what she'd heard from Toshie but took care not to mention the reporter or the perfume. It wouldn't do

Mizuho any favours to let them know she'd accepted a gift from someone in the press, even if it had been forced into her hands. Once this was done, Tomoko moved on to her questions.

'How was Mizuho yesterday?'

'Over the moon. You saw her, right, Sniffer?'

'I know she was fine when I saw her. But what about later in the day? Did anything happen at work?'

'Don't think so. She seemed happy right up until she left. Right, Yuasa?'

'Absolutely.'

Yuasa seemed to be a sensitive man, at least in comparison to the boorish Morishima. He looked genuinely distraught that one of his team had gone missing. He agreed that nothing major had taken place and that Mizuho had left the office at around six.

'Did she say anything about stopping off somewhere on the way?'

'No, not particularly.'

She'd left headquarters at six and nothing had seemed out of the ordinary at that point. That left a four-hour window between six and ten. Whatever had happened to wipe the smile from her face, it would have happened then. Perhaps she'd met up with someone. Perhaps the reporter. Tomoko suspected it wouldn't be easy to fill in the gaps. She could have extracted more information, perhaps, if Mizuho had had other female colleagues, but she was the only woman in Forensics. There had been two, sometimes even three, stationed here in the past. But Futawatari's plan to distribute the female officers more widely across the prefecture had left just one slot. Her own proposal to reshuffle these allocations, submitted that morning, had questioned whether this was, in fact, the best way of doing things.

Ceasefire, remember?

She tried to drive Futawatari from her mind.

Still . . . I could use this as a case in point.

She scolded herself for even entertaining the idea. She already had good reasons with which to argue against the individual posting of female officers. They were left isolated. And that increased their chances of becoming tokens like Junko Hayashi. *That* was what she wanted him to understand.

Returning to the present, Tomoko turned to face Yuasa. 'How's she been doing, in your assessment?'

'Good, very good. She works hard. Gets on with her team. I haven't seen anything to suggest any problems. I mean, you know, there's always the fact that she's—' Yuasa caught himself mid-sentence. His expression seemed to suggest he'd just realised who Tomoko was.

That she's . . .

The rest was obvious enough: *That she's a woman, so who's to say what she's really thinking?* There was a part of Tomoko that couldn't help agreeing. She thought about this as she made her way back downstairs. It was true that it was sometimes a challenge to judge what the officers under her purview were thinking. They were all women who had decided to join the force. As such, they were generally level-headed and in possession of a greater-than-average drive to contribute to society. Yet she couldn't deny that, with every passing year, she found it increasingly difficult to understand their motivations.

She couldn't help it. It was something she felt in her bones.

She didn't doubt that she was changing, too. She still considered herself one of them, but the truth of the matter was that she was now on the side of management, in charge of overseeing their forty-eight-strong headcount. She did, of course, try to see things from their perspective but she would also take the interests of the force into account when making any kind of decision. Even now, as she tried to understand what it was that Mizuho was going through, there was a part of her that was hoping to minimise potential damage to the force.

Shirota raised his hand when she arrived back in Administration. He pointed a finger towards Akama's office. As she made her way to the door, Tomoko thought she could already smell the cloying spice of the man's cologne.

5

'Am I right, Officer Nanao, to assume we're not yet treating this as a case?' Akama enquired in his usual smooth tone.

'Not at this point in time.'

'Does she have a boyfriend?' Akama said, holding up his ring finger.

'Not that I'm aware of, sir,' Tomoko answered, before averting her gaze.

She felt herself shiver. The gold-rimmed glasses, the tailored suit. The expensive cologne. Akama liked to play up to his image as one of the Tokyo elite but the man could still be appallingly crude. Three others had been called in with her: Chief Shirota of Administration, Chief Ogino of Welfare and Chief Takegami of Internal Affairs. A one-to-one conversation with a female officer was not something Akama's pride would permit.

'And what's she like – I mean, really like – in her job?'

'Highly conscientious, sir. No absences to date. She's reliable, definitely not the type to just give up and she takes pride in her work.' The words came easily. Current situation notwith-standing, this was the Mizuho she knew.

'Her type's the most vulnerable. They lack the necessary defences,' Akama said, looking satisfied with his analysis.

There's no telling what might happen when there's a man involved.

Love makes them crazy. Crazy enough to sacrifice everything they've worked for.

Akama was the kind of man who would take such statements at face value, not even thinking to question them. It was true that Tomoko had herself wondered whether there might be a man behind Mizuho's disappearance. She suspected it even now, whether it was the reporter or not. Yet in her mind all this signified was a recognition that relationships could, every now and then, break through the barriers of common sense and reason. It did not signify a one-sided belief that such things occurred only to women.

There were plenty of cases where the opposite was true.

She knew, of course, that nothing could be done to change Akama. Not long after his appointment to the role, he had asked her for the list of female officers in the prefecture.

You have forty-eight? Why so many? It was a single-digit number at my last post. I suggest you look into getting some of these girls a husband.

There was a cap on the number of officers a prefecture could enrol at any given time. This was governed by a ratio which took into account the general population. Despite an increase in crime and the number of calls requesting police assistance, the ratio had not changed in years. This left the force struggling to meet the demands made on them. A further issue with the cap was that it made no special provision for female officers. Every one of them, then, meant that one less male could be brought in. *They're better at the details.* There were executives who reeled off such niceties in public, even as they griped about the situation in private. *They're difficult to manage. It's a man's job to keep the peace.* Having been in the force for a while, Tomoko knew exactly how deep-rooted such opinions could be.

Yet she had never come across anyone who expressed their

prejudice quite as openly as Akama. He would of course hope that nothing serious had happened to Mizuho. But he would also be considering using the incident as ammunition to rid himself of a female officer. Tomoko couldn't help suspecting, based on the man's outward calm, that this was the case.

'Good. Let's keep an eye on developments.'

Akama was getting up from the couch when Futawatari knocked and came straight in.

'We found Mizuho's car.'

There was silence.

'Where?' Tomoko asked, the words catching in her throat.

'Parked outside Train Station M.'

Tomoko didn't know how to respond. *Train Station M.* That was where the gang leader had snatched the elderly woman's bag. The fear she'd dismissed, that of Mizuho having become involved in something dangerous, came rushing back. She hurried out after Futawatari. Her head was a mess. What had Mizuho been thinking? What had she been trying to accomplish? Could she be in some kind of danger?

Let her be safe.

The words hadn't come from her status as a fellow officer of the law, nor from her position as management. They had come, instead, from her natural instinct to protect a daughter.

6

'I can drive.'

'It's fine. We're almost there.'

Perhaps it was Futawatari's unparalleled talent for managing risk that had compelled him to sit behind the wheel. It was true that Tomoko had been in no state to drive when they'd left the building.

'Do you . . .'

'Mmm?'

'Do you think the bike gang might be involved?'

'It's hard to say at this point.'

'It's just that I was a bit concerned. After reading the articles this morning.'

'Understandable.'

Tomoko had expected Futawatari to agree but his response seemed unexpectedly muted. Did he have a theory of his own?

He brought the vehicle around, joining the roundabout in front of the station. Tomoko caught sight of Mizuho's red car. The van belonging to Mobile Forensics was parked next to it. Morishima was there, too.

'I'm getting out.'

Tomoko hopped from the not quite stationary vehicle and began to jog towards the cars.

'Sir!'

'That was quick, Sniffer.'

Mizuho's car was parked at the edge of the drop-off area.

'How long has it been here?'

'Not quite two hours, according to those guys.'

Morishima jutted his chin in the direction of a substation located some thirty metres down the road. His team having just arrived, Yuasa and the others were still unloading their equipment from the van. Headquarters wouldn't usually mobilise for a case like this but this was one of their own so they'd no doubt decided they couldn't leave it in the hands of district.

Tomoko began to inspect the car. She remembered the drill. The first step was to observe from a distance. There was nothing to suggest it had come to a sudden stop. It was flush with the kerb and the front wheels were neatly aligned. There were no visible scratches or dents and the side mirrors were angled correctly. She took a walk around the chassis, checking each of the windows. No cracks, and no sign of blood.

'Make sure you don't touch anything.'

At Morishima's warning, Tomoko drew her head away from the glass. She scanned the area. Footfall was high. The drop-off point was in open view. It wasn't, she thought, a viable spot to abduct a grown woman.

'Here.'

Yuasa's team gathered around the car. With a practised hand, he used a standard-issue metal wire to open the lock.

'Mind if I go first?'

Tomoko pushed her way to the front. If Pomade or Hair Oil moved in before her, she'd lose her chance to get a good whiff of the interior.

Morishima put on a pair of white gloves then opened the front door, cautioning that she was to use nothing apart from her nose. Tomoko leaned in and angled her head. She'd expected Chanel but her nose bristled at something unexpected. *Cigarettes.* The smell was faint but unmistakeable. It was her least favourite smell. She took another sniff, moving in until her nose was almost touching the driver's seat. Still there was no hint of perfume. Could it have faded with time? Been overpowered by the tobacco? It was possible, she supposed, that Mizuho hadn't been wearing any to begin with. The smell had been there in her room but no one had confirmed that she'd been wearing any when she'd left the dorm that morning.

'Anything?'

Morishima called out from behind. Tomoko turned around and asked if they would open the ashtray. Yuasa obliged, sliding the drawer open. Two stubs. Mild Seven. The filters were unmarked, no traces of lipstick. *The reporter?* Tomoko's thoughts raced as Morishima and the others exchanged looks. They looked a little let down.

'Really? A man?'

Tomoko put her head inside for a second time. This time she ignored any smells and used her eyes instead.

Angle of rear-view mirror? *Good.* Sun visors? *Stowed.* Mats and upholstery? *Clean.* Anything easily missed, maybe a good-luck charm, on the floor? *Nothing.* Visible bloodstains? *None.*

'Time's up, Sniffer.'

The driver's seat was positioned close to the wheel. Too narrow for a man, barring someone who was exceptionally small. Which meant that Mizuho had been driving . . .

Morishima took Tomoko by the shoulder and tugged her out of the circle of officers. It was only then, as her body relaxed, that she realised how tense she'd become. Mizuho hadn't been abducted. There were the cigarette butts, sure, making it more or less certain that a man had been in there with her, yet there was nothing to suggest that anything untoward had taken place. If a struggle had taken place, there were always signs, but Tomoko hadn't found any. Not one. Mizuho had driven to the station, parked her car, locked the doors and walked away. With the man who smoked the Mild Seven. Either that, or she'd come here alone with a view to meeting him later. What seemed certain was that she'd come here to the station. The parking area served the station and the station alone. Which meant she'd probably boarded a train. The Shitetsu line ran east to west, and she could switch midway to a JR train and head north or south. Those trains could take her outside the prefecture.

Tomoko's head reeled at the thought. She realised she hadn't yet eaten lunch. She angled her wrist to check her watch. It was already three thirty.

I should get something in my stomach.

She walked to the first shop she could see and picked up a random selection of pastries. She was about to head back to the station when she saw a phone box. Still edgy from nerves, she punched in a number. The unwelcome sound of her own voice came on after a few rings, informing her that she was out.

She left a brief message.

'Yacho. I'm going to be late. There's curry in the freezer.'

She put the phone down and noticed Futawatari standing behind her, holding a can of coffee.

'Your son is in year nine?'

'Year ten, now,' Tomoko answered, blushing a little.

'So he's got exams. That'll be tough on the lad.'

'Yes, well, he's kind of given up on them. Your daughter, she . . .?'

'Started secondary school this spring. She's cheeky, always looking for trouble.'

Futawatari had already heard from Morishima that there was nothing in the car to suggest that a crime had taken place. He told Tomoko he was going back to headquarters and asked what she was planning. She considered waiting but thought she would be too conspicuous in her uniform. Forensics, too, would be a while yet. She told him she'd come back with him, at least for the time being, and took the wheel for the return journey.

'How did it go at the bank?'

'She hasn't touched her account. No activity at all.'

'Meaning she can't have gone far.'

'Perhaps. Although she could probably take money out en route, if she needs it.'

'And she might not even need to, if she's with someone.'

'Yes.'

Not for the first time, Futawatari's reaction seemed a little muted. Perhaps he'd already concluded that Mizuho was by herself. That would be perfectly normal. He didn't know about the perfume in her room or about the reporter who had given it to her. Tomoko began to worry that his judgement was being affected by the lack of information. She should probably bring him up to speed. There'd been the development of the cigarettes in the car, too. Considering there were no other men she knew about in Mizuho's life, she decided it was probably time to mention the reporter.

'Sir . . .'

She told Futawatari everything she had learned: about the perfume and about the man. Futawatari did seem a little surprised but his tone was as relaxed as before when he answered.

'I suppose we should look into that.'

Tomoko changed in the locker room before returning to Administration, where she saw Press Director Genichi Funaki at Futawatari's desk. The two men were locked in a heated discussion.

'What if it turns out not to be the reporter? Look, we have to be careful. If the press catch wind of the fact that Officer Hirano has gone missing . . .'

Tomoko caught the man's trademark body odour as she over-heard part of their conversation. Funaki was a contemporary of Futawatari's. Equally aggressive in their pursuit of advancement, they had made inspector together. Yet Futawatari's promotion to superintendent had come two years ahead of his colleague's. Their relationship, Tomoko had heard, had never been the same since. This made it difficult to gauge how much the press direc-tor's refusal to cooperate stemmed from his fear of tipping off the press and how much from his personal issues with Futawatari.

Tomoko bit into a pastry, using her free hand to pull out a binder marked 'Female Officers Network'. Inside were the phone numbers of all forty-eight female officers posted across the head-quarters and the prefecture's seventeen district stations. She had decided it would be useful in gathering more information on Mizuho. Tomoko had hesitated until now, not wanting to be the source of gossip, but it was already four thirty. She couldn't allow herself to sit back and do nothing while she waited for Mizuho to return.

She dialled the first number on the list.

Police Sergeant Saito. Criminal Investigations. Station W.

Officer Saito had worked with Tomoko in Administration until her transfer out last year.

'I'd like you to make some calls.'

Tomoko brought Saito up to speed, leaving her with instructions to call the officers at the substation near Train Station M if she learned anything new, anything at all. Putting the phone down, Tomoko turned around.

Futawatari and Funaki were still sniping at each other.

'You must know the brands your reporters smoke. You *are* the press director?'

'Of course I am. That's why I'm telling you: this is dangerous.'

Tomoko waited for an opening then informed Futawatari that she was going back to the train station. She left the office and walked down the corridor. Making quick work of the stairs, she left via the building's main entrance. It was already growing dark outside, mirroring the half-light inside the building.

Tomoko kept her foot on the accelerator and arrived at the station just as the Mobile Forensics team were packing up.

'Watch duty, Sniffer?'

'That's right.'

'Tough break.'

She sat on a pavement bench a little away from the drop-off point. It was now past five thirty. Crowds emerged from the station every fifteen to twenty minutes, indicating the start of the evening rush. The majority were in dark suits, so a cream dress would stand out.

Where on earth are you?

It was dark by seven. With most of the cars gone, Mizuho's was left by itself. Once she was confident she'd grasped the timing of the trains, Tomoko got to her feet. She walked to the phone box outside the store and dialled the number for home.

'Hello?' The uninterested tone of her son's voice, recently broken, was just like his father's.

'Yacho. Have you had dinner yet?'

'Stop calling me that,' he protested.

'Sorry. *Ya-chi-o*. Look, I'm going to be late after all.'

'. . .'

'Are you still there?'

'Yes.'

'Try to get some studying done, won't you?'

The line clicked off.

Her watch showed eight, then nine, and still there was no sign of Mizuho. Time seemed to slow to a crawl as she waited there alone. She realised it would be the same for her son. Waiting was the only constant he'd had, growing up.

Tomoko checked her watch again, noting the time as nine thirty when an officer in uniform jogged up to her from the substation. They'd had a call from one of her female officers, a Mitsuko Adachi from Juvenile Crime in headquarters. She'd called after hearing of Mizuho's disappearance via the network.

'This is Tomoko. Do you have something for me, Officer Adachi?'

'Yes. I saw Mizuho's car, early this morning.'

'Her car? Where?'

The news came as a shock. Mitsuko went on to tell Tomoko that she'd seen Mizuho's car a little before eight that morning, parked outside the Prefectural HQ. *I'm pretty sure it was her. She always parks in the same spot and the grille kind of stands out.* Her tone had left little room for doubt. Tomoko found it hard to regain her calm, even after she ended the call.

Mizuho had come to work. She'd made it as far as the parking area but driven off instead of coming in.

It didn't make sense.

Tomoko slumped back into her metal chair inside the substation. She could at least be certain now that Mizuho had not made her decision to disappear until early that morning. She'd been out of sorts the previous evening, perhaps, but she'd come all the way to the Prefectural HQ. She'd intended to come to work as usual. Something had happened in the parking area to change her mind. But what? Had Mild Seven called her while she was in the car? That didn't seem likely. As far as Tomoko knew, Mizuho didn't own a mobile phone. Which left . . . what? Tomoko felt suddenly afraid, as though she'd peered into an old, dark well.

'Excuse me. Sir?'

' . . '

'Sir . . .?'

Coming back to herself, Tomoko looked around to see the officer in uniform once again holding up his phone.

'We've just been informed that Officer Hirano is back with her family.'

8

Her hurt and concern were mixed with relief, leaving Tomoko confused as to what it was she was supposed to be feeling. She pressed on the accelerator and made sure it stayed down. There was no point in hurrying but there was nothing she could do to stop herself.

What the hell had it all been about?

Mizuho's home was located deep in the mountains. Tomoko had been there before, when she'd first met her parents, and for certain administrative tasks, but this was the first time she'd had to make the trip at night. The area was mostly farming villages, all alike, and there were no street lights or signposts worthy of the name. The date was on the verge of changing when, after a good deal of backtracking, Tomoko finally reached her destination.

The main building had a thatched roof with a chimney and had probably been used for sericulture in the past. Lights were on in the building next to it, a two-storey home with stone walls. Mizuho's mother appeared, head dipped in apology, when Tomoko called from the entrance. She kept repeating that she was sorry then turned to call for her daughter, barely managing to conceal her anger.

'Mizuho, could you come to the door?'

A cream dress appeared at the end of the hallway. At first, the impression was that of something inanimate. Mizuho shuffled forwards, her eyes and nose red. It seemed she'd been crying for a while.

Mizuho . . .

Tomoko breathed a deep sigh of relief. She set her chin and filled her lungs before looking up again. 'I'm so glad you're safe.' The anger was gone. All that remained was a boundless sense of relief.

'Officer Nanao . . .' In the hallway, Mizuho's voice sounded brittle. Nasal and congested, it was the voice of someone trying not to burst into tears.

Tomoko fought her own urge to cry. She found herself pulling Mizuho into a tight hug. 'Silly. You had us all worried.'

'I'm really sorry.'

'Where on earth have you been?'

In place of an answer, Mizuho buried her face in Tomoko's chest. She smelled of sweat. Tomoko understood. It was hard work to cry.

Entering the front room, Tomoko saw Morishima next to Mizuho's father, the two men looking deadly serious. She'd seen the former's car so had known he would be there.

Mizuho huddled up next to her mother.

'She refuses to tell us what this is all about.' The woman gave her daughter a look of total exasperation. Yet she did not let go of Mizuho's hand, continuing every now and then to massage her fingers.

Mizuho's head stayed down. Her expression was like stone, devoid of emotion.

'*Mizuho!*' Her father, cigarette smouldering and tipped in the direction of the floor, yelled her name.

'Perhaps we can reconvene another time,' Morishima suggested before Tomoko had a chance to interject. 'It's late and Mizuho should get some rest. We should probably call it a night, too, Officer Nanao?'

Tomoko nodded. She desperately wanted to know what was going on inside Mizuho's head but realised it was probably futile, at this stage, to keep trying for information. She was happy enough to celebrate the fact that Mizuho was home and safe.

'Give me a call when you feel better.'

'. . .'

'I'll take you for that *anmitsu* I promised.'

'Good, good,' Morishima grumbled. He gave Tomoko a look that told her it was time to leave.

They got to their feet and Mizuho stood, too, angling herself into a deep bow. Tomoko caught sight of a framed photo behind her. A beaming smile, standing in salute before one of the prefecture's substations.

Mizuho came with them to the door, keeping in the shadow of her parents. For a moment, Tomoko thought she saw a pleading look on the girl's face.

An incredible number of stars greeted them as they left. Walking back to their cars, Tomoko dropped her voice to a whisper. 'Did she come back alone?'

'Yes.'

'On the train?'

'That's right. She got on at Train Station M. Called home when she got to the station closest to here.'

'It's strange, though. Why not just drive here?'

'Who knows?' Morishima said, sounding uninterested as he clambered into his car.

It was all still a mystery.

Perhaps Mizuho *had* suffered a broken heart. Tomoko had never seen the girl looking so dejected. Halfway into her seat,

Tomoko turned back towards the house. On the first floor, the lights had come on. She thought she could sense Mizuho looking out from the bedroom window.

Get some sleep.

Tomoko managed the return trip without getting lost, making it home in just forty minutes. It was already two in the morning. The lights were on in the hallway, the front room and the bathroom. The TV was on, too.

No different to usual.

She crept forwards and poked her head into the back room. Yachio was asleep on the bed, still fully clothed. He looked as innocent as he had as a toddler, when, unable to properly pronounce his name, he'd proudly told her that 'Yacho' was doing this and 'Yacho' was doing that. His textbooks were strewn across the floor. His desk held his TV, stereo and computer, along with enough games and CDs to start a business. They were what he used to pass the time. To fill the gaps. To alleviate the worry.

I'll make it up to him, one day.

She'd been saying it for fifteen years.

She rearranged his sheets and went back to the front room. She warmed some curry and ate it with some bread.

She started to cry.

Her son, the female officers for whom she was responsible – they were all so far away. When she tried to help, they resisted. Knocked her back. Left her by herself. She felt betrayed by the ring on her finger. It could do nothing to help. It had no answers.

The morning paper was still there on the table. *Female Officer's Triumph.* Mizuho was looking out at her, dressed in uniform.

Mizuho. Talk to me.

The perfume. The cigarettes. The reporter.

The images swirled randomly through her tired head. First the perfume. She'd picked up the scent in Mizuho's room, yet it hadn't been there in the car. Nor had she noticed it earlier, when she'd hugged Mizuho close. There'd been the smell of sweat but nothing to suggest the girl had been wearing perfume. Perhaps she hadn't used it on herself. Perhaps she'd sprayed it, but only around her room.

Why?

Maybe it had been someone else. Someone other than Mizuho. But who? And why? The urge to sleep was becoming too strong. Tomoko decided to stop fighting it.

Time for bed.

Whatever happened, she would pay Mizuho another visit the following day. She got to her feet, cleared away the empty plates and was about to fold the paper in two when her hands came to an abrupt stop. A sentence from the page caught her attention. Something wasn't right. She kept reading, unable to pin the feeling down. Her vision began to blur. She started again, this time scanning the article from the top. She read the whole thing, word by word.

Her eyes opened wide.

No . . .

As the understanding dawned on her, she remembered Mizuho's pleading look. A hypothesis formed in her mind. The various fragments of information in her head began to slot together, as though they'd always been part of the same puzzle. The perfume, too, fitted in neatly among them. The hypothesis became fact.

But that's . . .

Tomoko looked again at Mizuho's drawing. The lines seemed darker, blacker than before. Her knees started to tremble. She tried to steady them but her hand began to tremble with them. A shudder ran through her.

The conclusion she'd come to, the cruel act she'd seen in her mind's eye was, in fact, the answer she'd been looking for.

9

It was, she discovered, surprisingly hard to justify a private meeting with a man who wasn't your husband or partner, especially when the man in question was a member of the police. Having exhausted her options, Tomoko had finally opted to hold the secret talk in the station itself, and during the day. Her meeting was with Pomade, the bulldog.

She lowered her voice. 'The likeness was far from accurate. At first.'

'. . .'

'That's why you ordered her to redo it.'

'What if I did?' Morishima retorted, settling back to let the couch take his weight.

He was clearly not planning to take this gracefully; the man seemed more annoyed than anything else. Tomoko had expected him to become defensive. If he'd been the kind of man who could apologise, he would never have issued such a callous order in the first place. He genuinely believed that it was no big deal.

Tomoko had spent a week looking into what had happened.

The starting point had come when she'd re-read the article and realised the shocking contradiction it contained.

It hadn't been possible.

Mizuho could never have drawn something so accurate. The

victim had had her bag snatched. At seventy, she was elderly, and it would all have been over in an instant. She could never have been expected to recall the man's features to any degree of accuracy. It wouldn't matter how talented Mizuho was at asking the right questions, or at drawing, when there was no foundation on which to work.

No one had noticed, of course, amidst the excitement of the arrest and the shop owner's claim that the drawing was a perfect, spitting image.

Why had he said such a thing to begin with?

He'd feared the gang leader for some time. All day, the man rode around in a pimped-up car, stinking of solvent abuse. *He's trouble*. The owner would have already suspected that something was likely to happen. Then the police had turned up bearing a likeness, saying the man in the drawing was the instigator of a theft. Maybe it was the shape of the hair, perhaps the contours of the face – something in the picture would have been close enough. The owner had become convinced it was the man from the gang.

There was another factor, too, which had been a factor in the shop owner's choice of words. The man in question had only ever bought pornography at the store. It was standard practice, in such cases, for staff to avoid eye contact to reduce the shame of the customer.

The owner had never properly seen the man's face, not up close.

His words had set everything in motion.

Forensics had been notified in the morning that the likeness had led to an arrest. Knowing it would look good for the division, Morishima had called Media Relations to arrange a press conference. When the photo of the man eventually arrived from district, however, he'd realised that the resemblance was scant at best. He'd panicked. The press conference was already set for the evening. He'd handed the photo to Mizuho and requested that she redraw the likeness. She'd refused. She'd told him she couldn't do it, over and over. He'd lost his temper and shouted the words.

This is why we don't need women in the force.

That was what had broken her. She'd never complained when she'd rushed to crime scenes in the dead of night. She'd always been the first to help carry the team's heavy equipment. She'd poured plaster on footprints, ignoring the urge to pee even as her team mates relieved themselves by the side of the road. She had never once protested.

Despite this, she'd been pigeon-holed as a 'woman'. She'd been told she wasn't needed.

She'd agreed to do it. Her mind had been blank as her hands moved over the paper, mechanically following the method she'd been taught. Morishima had been overjoyed with the result. The reporters, too, had jumped on the chance to write up the story of her accomplishment.

Mizuho alone had been crushed, hating herself for the deception. The next day she'd made it as far as the parking area but that had been her limit. She'd tried her best but she hadn't been able to come into the office. She no longer deserved the uniform. She thought herself a disgrace.

Morishima, the man responsible for all of this, now sat before Tomoko. He was smoking a cigarette but not enjoying it, tapping his foot just loudly enough to make it a challenge.

'It was you who sprayed the perfume in her room.'

Morishima had been spooked when Mizuho had failed to show the next day. He'd called the dorm but that hadn't been enough to allay his fears so he'd headed there in person. He was afraid she might have left a note that detailed what he'd asked her to do. He would be in trouble if anyone saw such a thing.

But there hadn't been a note. He'd been relieved but had noticed a potential complication at the same time. He, more than anyone, knew about Tomoko's keen sense of smell – he'd been the one, after all, to first call her Sniffer. He also knew that she was in charge of looking after the prefecture's female officers. She would visit the dorm if she heard Mizuho was missing. If she did, she would notice the smell of his pomade.

He'd left for the dorm at nine, a time when Mizuho's absence could have still been written off as tardiness. Not only that, he'd gone there in person and gone into her room despite the ban on men entering the dorm. He'd realised this would make Tomoko suspicious so he'd opened the window to flush out the smell. Worried this wasn't enough, he'd seen the bottle of perfume and sprayed it around for good measure. Finally, he'd cajoled Toshie into keeping his secret on the pretext that Mizuho would hate to find out he'd been in her room.

He'd returned to Forensics, waited a decent amount of time then called Tomoko to give her the news.

'Anything to say for yourself?'

'This is a joke. You're being naive.'

'. . .'

'We can't have our officers wandering off each time there's a minor setback. To be honest, this whole thing is really—'

There was a sharp *clap*. Morishima's eyes widened with shock. Tomoko's hand was already back on her knee.

'If you'll excuse me, sir.'

She got to her feet. She'd already weighed up the risks. Morishima wouldn't dare tell a soul that a female officer had slapped him in the face. She walked out of Forensics. She turned once on her way out but the man hadn't moved from his place behind the partition.

The meeting had done nothing to brighten her mood. It wasn't just Morishima. There was Yuasa, too, and all the other members of Mizuho's team. They would all have known that she'd redone the drawing. So, too, would the detectives who'd brought the man in. Not one of them had spoken up. From her disappearance to the moment she was found at home, no one had thought to say a damn thing.

It was unnerving.

The corridor seemed to shrink around her. Tomoko picked up speed, her shoes clicking loudly on the floor. She took off her ring and held it tightly in her fist. For the first time, she understood she had no choice but to make superintendent.

As she made the trip almost daily, the dogs and free-roaming chickens of the farm no longer seemed to regard Tomoko as an outsider.

'You can take some time off. It's been approved,' Tomoko said, stroking the muzzle of the cow next to her.

'I'm not sure that I'll, you know . . .' Mizuho's eyes dropped to the ground. She was wearing denim overalls and oversized wellies. They suited her.

'Don't decide anything now. Take your time and think it over.'

'Thanks.'

On the day she went missing Mizuho had walked. She'd visited a café, a bookstore, another café. But she was a girl with a strong sense of duty and there was only so much time she could spend doing nothing. What she did next proved beyond a shadow of doubt that she was police.

She decided she needed to know why it was that someone had claimed her drawing to be a spitting image of the assailant, even though nothing could have been further from the truth. Caught up in celebrating the arrest, she'd forgotten to ask who had given the statement. And the papers had described the man only as owning a shop, not revealing his name in case the gang sought retaliation.

Feeling guilty for not having gone into work, Mizuho had decided she couldn't contact anyone in the force. The reporter who'd given her the perfume had come to mind. She'd called him in his office and asked for the name of the shop. He'd come to see her in person. The Mild Sevens in the car had been his. Having learned this much, Mizuho had driven to Train Station M, where she'd parked, then walked into the shop. She'd been inside, talking to the owner, when the van belonging to Mobile Forensics had pulled up.

'I was shivering behind a display case when you came in to buy those pastries,' Mizuho said, showing the hint of a smile, perhaps the first since the day of her disappearance.

'Silly girl. I could have bought you some juice if you'd just told me.'

Anmitsu, soon, Tomoko told herself as she headed back to her car. She felt better now that Mizuho's leave had been officially sanctioned. Especially as the green light had come from Akama himself. She couldn't even begin to guess how Futawatari had made that happen.

Futawatari, for his part, had not asked for a report after Mizuho's return. He'd read the article several times. It was possible he'd worked out from the start that the likeness had been redone. That he'd conducted some kind of investigation of his own. If that were the case, his true colours would be revealed come the next transfer season. Would he choose to punish Morishima for his actions? Or would he choose to overlook them, write them off as unavoidable from the perspective of someone in charge?

For now, Tomoko had something else to focus on – the yellow folder that rested on the passenger seat. It contained her redrafted proposal to reassign the female officers in the prefecture.

She would hand it in the moment she got to the office.

She turned the wheel to join the prefectural highway, causing the eggs Mizuho had given her to rattle on the back seat.

BRIEFCASE

Once the morning had passed, you could hardly read without the aid of a desk light. While this was true for the whole of the Prefectural HQ, the ground and first floors that housed Administrative Affairs were particularly dark. The archives, which had been built just outside the windows, robbed them not only of sunlight but also of any kind of view. They'd been told to put up with it, at least until the new headquarters was ready, but a drop in tax revenues had meant budget cuts and the project itself had been put on hold for close to three years.

Dressed in a suit, his steps tapping a precise rhythm, Masaki Tsuge made his way down the cold underground passage. There were two ways to get to the Prefectural Government from the Prefectural HQ: either cross the bridge over the national highway or head underground. Tsuge preferred the latter. He didn't necessarily consider it a reflection of the way he worked but he knew he disliked the bridge and the way it left you exposed.

Administrative Affairs. Secretariat. Assistant Chief. Inspector. Thirty-six. In charge of Assembly Relations.

As he reached the top of the stairs, the government building came into view. With the tiles catching the sun, it resembled a vast office. The structure in front of it, an ultra-modern affair that looked like a concert hall, was the prefectural assembly. Both had been thrown up only five years earlier. Standing here served as a stark reminder of how the Prefectural HQ had been left behind.

I'll get the project moving again.

Tsuge began to walk towards the assembly. Slipping through the revolving doors, he peeked through the door of the office to the right. Civil servants bustled around the usually quiet room, twenty or so hurrying from one desk to the next. They were busy with the preparations for September's cabinet meeting.

Tsuge called out to a man he recognised. They would all know why he was there, so there was little to explain.

'Just remember these aren't final,' the man cautioned, handing across five stapled-together sheets of recycled paper.

The questions.

Tsuge set himself on a couch in the corner of the room and began to flip through the pages. Written inside were the names of those assembly members who were planning to take part in the question-and-answer session. Next to each was a box where they could indicate the subject matter. That was the reason Tsuge was here. During the meeting, the captain of the Prefectural HQ would stand as a member of the executive, ready to answer any questions about the police. Tsuge needed the information in these sheets so the police could draft his responses in advance.

He traced his finger carefully down the page.

Drugs and Legislation. This was in the box next to Assemblyman Oiso's name. Tsuge jotted a memo in his notebook. There was a new drug that had recently made the news for being a stimulant and difficult to regulate under current legislation. Tsuge felt his usual admiration for Oiso's keen eye.

Misaki was next. *Police.* That was all it said in his box. Usually that meant he intended to ask the police a question but had yet to decide on the content. But this was Misaki, so it was probably worth doing a double check.

Sakuma was the next name to be added to Tsuge's notebook. *The Elderly.* His box was clearly marked. Considering his track record, the topic would probably focus on how to help the elderly maintain a sense of purpose in society. Such questions often touched on the issue of suicide, which would require statistics and background analysis. In such cases, the captain of the Prefectural HQ would usually be expected to comment once the director of Welfare had said his piece.

Tsuge took a few final notes, feeling a sense of relief as he flicked the bundle of sheets closed. He hadn't seen anything that was inflammatory, nothing that attacked the captain. Even the opposition appeared to have forgone their usual jabs. The economy was bottoming out and the resultant growth in issues such as bankruptcy and unemployment had no doubt left them with little time for taking potshots at the force.

I should probably start with old-man Misaki.

Tsuge got to his feet. Stepping out of the room, he padded down thick carpet, aiming for the cavernous room at the far end of the corridor. *The New Liberal Democratic Club.* Its use was reserved for the members of the largest conservative faction. Misaki did not appear to be present. When Tsuge asked after him, the female attendant told him he was upstairs. Tsuge climbed the stairs to the second floor. Assembly members who had previously occupied the post of chairman or vice-chairman were allocated private rooms known as 'studies'.

'Could I bother you for a moment?'

'Ah, Tsuge. Perfect timing. I was about to call you.' Misaki's enormous frame looked as though it was part of the couch. The man had loosened his belt and sat with his zip half down, easing the pressure on the flab around his belly. His log-like legs were thrown over the desk. He was almost seventy but the eyes buried within his oily face contained the sparkle of a younger man's. 'You and I, we're always in sync.'

'Was it about this?' Tsuge held up the notebook and the spot where he'd written 'Police'.

Misaki gave a satisfied nod. 'What do you think I should ask?'

'Do you have any preferences?'

'I'd like something with . . . impact. Something that'll be a hit with the locals.'

The elections would follow soon after the cabinet meeting. Misaki no doubt wanted something that would help him earn some extra brownie points. Although . . . Tsuge brought to mind Misaki's unexpected struggle during the elections four years ago, against a newcomer who'd come in with the backing of a local citizens' group. And here he was, a seasoned politician, going out of his way to take part in the question-and-answer session. Perhaps he sensed danger.

If he doesn't have anything, maybe get him to ask about the delay in the renovation of the headquarters.

That had been Tsuge's plan, but he should perhaps reconsider. Whatever happened, he would need Misaki's backing to get the project underway. Tsuge changed tack. The smart move would be to build goodwill, give the man a question that was in line with his own agenda.

'What about drugs? I haven't done anything on drugs for a while.'

'Assemblyman Oiso has something on that. I think he's planning to bring up the legislation in the context of new drugs that are hard to regulate.'

'Well, that's no fun. Do me a favour and think something up, would you? Put that sharp mind of yours to use.'

As far as Tsuge knew, Misaki was the only member of the assembly who was willing to leave the content of his question to someone else. Not that he looked down on the man for it. Born into a poor family, Misaki had barely finished primary school. Despite this, he had managed in the space of a single generation to build himself a successful construction business then leverage his newfound capital to take a key role in the prefectural assembly.

Tsuge found his drive attractive, and he liked to think he saw something of himself in the way this man had lived his life.

What should he ask?

Tsuge considered the options as he made his way back along the underground passage. Misaki would no doubt charter a bus to ensure that the seats in the hall were filled with his supporters. Tsuge needed something to impress them. Leaving the passage, Tsuge recalled a fatal hit-and-run that had taken place in Misaki's electoral district just two weeks ago. If memory served, they had yet to make an arrest.

That might do it.

He climbed the stairs of the north building. Transport Guidance was located at the end of the corridor on the second floor. Flagging down Assistant Chief Yoshikawa, Tsuge enquired how the investigation was progressing.

'It's only a matter of time before we make an arrest. We got the model of the car from a sample of paint. It's a Bluebird. White. There are a lot of cars matching that description so it'll take a bit of time, of course. I'd say around a month.'

'Assemblyman Misaki wants to ask a question about it during the next session. Any problem if the captain tells him we know the car's a Bluebird?'

'I'd welcome it. If it gets to the press, whoever it is will realise they're going to be caught. A lot of people turn themselves in at that point.'

Done.

The decision was made. Misaki would enquire as to the status of the hit-and-run incident. The captain would give a standard response, something about having officers on the case, about being committed to hunting down the culprit, but he would also add the flourish of the car being a Bluebird. For Misaki, that would be a win. The force, too, would have nothing to lose. The comment would pressure the perpetrator to come in, and Tsuge happened to know that the arrest rate for this type of case was close to a hundred per cent. The captain could mention that at the same time and secure some good PR for the force.

Tsuge took some papers from Yoshikawa then made his way back to the Secretariat on the first floor of the main building. Despite the fact that this was his home in the Prefectural HQ, he still felt nervous each time he walked in. The captain's private office was behind the door at the back. The lamp that indicated whether he was present was off. Even without this, the lack of bustle would have been enough to let him know that the captain was away from his post. He checked with the secretary, Aiko Toda, who told him the captain was out for lunch with the chief and the members of the Public Safety Committee. Looking at his watch, Tsuge saw that it was almost noon.

You can get it done before they get back.

He ordered some udon then sat at his desk and lifted the screen of his word processor. He set about drafting the question for Misaki. The usual format would be to open with some commentary on the state of road safety in general then move on to discuss the hit-and-run case:

An increase in traffic has brought about an equivalent rise in dangerous driving. I do not take any joy in saying this, but I believe there has been a gradual yet consistent decline in the standards we uphold for our . . .

Tsuge made the finishing touches as he ate his lunch. He stamped the document, checked it once more then added phonetics to help with the more difficult characters.

Good.

Tsuge asked Aiko, back from lunch, to make some copies then left the Secretariat once this had been done. He handed the paper to Transport Guidance and Planning and asked them to put together a response for the captain.

Misaki will like this.

Feeling more at ease, Tsuge returned to the office just as a call came in from the assemblyman.

'Tsuge, how's it coming along?'

'I think I've found something suitable. I'll bring you the paper tomorrow.'

'Fantastic. Much appreciated.'

'Not at all.'

'I guess I should repay the favour. Here, let me give you some news.'

'News?'

'I take it you know Ukai?'

Assemblyman Ukai. Vice-representative for the New Wave Party, the second-largest conservative faction.

'The assemblyman?'

'Yes. So, anyway, I heard he's sitting on a time bomb.'

'A bomb?'

'Indeed. One he plans to set off during the questions. Seems it's for the police.'

Tsuge felt his hair stand on end.

2

Tsuge tried not to stumble as he scrambled down the underground passage. He raced into the room next to the entrance of the assembly and, gasping for air, scanned the list of questions a second time. He found Ukai's name. *Environmental hormones. Support for Small and Medium Businesses.* Two subjects, and nothing to indicate any questions for the police. Was Ukai planning to ask something without telling them first? Something that was potentially explosive? Tsuge couldn't stop a shiver from running down his spine. He saw an image of the captain, alone in the assembly hall, lost for words. For a man like Tsuge, whose role was to manage relations with the prefectural assembly, it signified nothing less than the end of his career. What could Ukai be planning to ask? And why would he want to attack the Prefectural HQ?

Revenge.

There was a reason for Tsuge's gut feeling. *Ichiro Ukai. Fifty-six.* Elected for five straight terms and having served as vice-chairman in the assembly, the man was a key figure in local government. Despite this, his faction had been investigated on charges of bribery during the last election, charges which had resulted in the arrest of fifteen members of his campaign. While the investigation had been instigated by the Office of the District Prosecutor, Second Division had still taken it as a badge of pride to raid, for the first time, the camp of a man as high-standing as Ukai. For Ukai, the number-two man in the conservative factions, the investigation would have been a calamity, and it was hard to imagine the anger and humiliation he must have felt at having his reputation dragged through the mud.

Even so, to actually seek revenge . . .

There was a delicate balance of power between the assembly and the force. While they were outwardly cooperative, each had the strength to keep the other in check, the police by investigative means, the assembly by legislative. Each worked to suppress the other. And while this promoted a certain rivalry, the hoped-for outcome was peaceful cohabitation, just as it was with any nuclear deterrent. What, then, would happen if someone in the assembly chose to act on a personal grudge? The police would retaliate during the next cycle. The assembly would respond by flexing its legislative muscles, launching a counterstrike. The chain of reprisal would continue ad infinitum. Such an arrangement would benefit nobody. It was because this was fully understood that such actions were considered taboo.

But Ukai was planning something nevertheless.

That left the question of scale. What had he managed to lay his hands on? Had he perhaps dug up an illegal flow of funds? Some kind of corruption? Found some dirt he could pin on a member of the executive? It was now Tsuge's number-one priority to find out what it was. Only then could he enter negotiations with a view to defusing the situation, or, failing that, begin to formulate a viable response.

Tsuge set off for the club room belonging to the New Wave Party. He put his head around the door and looked inside. Ukai didn't seem to be there. He saw Sakuma, sitting by himself at the back of the room, and hurried over.

'Assemblyman.'

'Tsuge.'

At forty, Sakuma was currently in his second year with the assembly. He was modest, despite his formidable intellect. Tsuge took a seat beside him. He already had something he wanted to ask the man, so decided to open with that.

'Will you be needing anything from the police for your question on the elderly?'

'Possibly, yes. I was going to ask for some information on suicides. Would that be something—'

'First Division, Autopsy. They can help with that; they manage the numbers.'

'Perfect. Do they keep notes on the underlying reasons?'

'I think so, in most cases. I'll check on that and get back to you.' Maintaining his expression, Tsuge lowered his voice. 'I'm actually looking for Assemblyman Ukai. Do you know if he's in today?'

'I haven't seen him, no, although it's possible he's upstairs.'

Tsuge brought his voice down to a whisper. 'I heard he's planning to ask something police-related.'

'Yes, I think I remember him saying something like that.'

'Do you know what he's planning to ask?'

'He said you wouldn't like it, but, no, he didn't give me any details.'

So it was true. Ukai had something he was planning to use against the force.

'I'll ask if I see him. Can't have you worrying too much.'

'Thank you. That would be a great help.' Tsuge bowed his head and told the man he'd call later that night. He bowed one more time.

Next was the New Liberal Democratic Club. In the case of the assembly, it often happened that the opposition was privy to the same – or more – information as the party in power.

The trip earned him no new knowledge but everyone he approached seemed to know something about Ukai's intention to launch an offensive.

I've got to find Ukai.

The decision wasn't a hard one. Tsuge had no particular fear of confronting the man. He could be a little difficult, a little obtuse, but Tsuge had no issues with his type. In the course of the last six months Tsuge considered himself to have built a decent enough relationship with the man. Perhaps he'd missed something, or perhaps Ukai was more cunning than he'd thought. It would have to be one of the two, if he truly was planning something.

Tsuge climbed to the second floor and knocked on the door to the assemblyman's study. There was no answer.

'Assemblyman?'

Tsuge swallowed then pushed on the door. There was no one inside. A briefcase on the desk, however, told Tsuge the man was somewhere in the building. The door was half closed when something compelled Tsuge to stop. His eyes flicked back to the desk. To the brown and well-worn briefcase. It was open. Papers poked out from the inside.

No . . .

Tsuge had to catch his breath. He closed the door. In that moment, he heard a voice behind him.

'Can I be of assistance?'

Tsuge flinched as he turned to see Ukai standing in the corridor, looking wary. The small towel in his hands meant he'd been visiting the bathroom.

'Assemblyman. Sorry, I thought you were in your study.'

Ukai held Tsuge's gaze, his pin-like eyes sharpening behind black-rimmed glasses. Tsuge felt a rising panic. It was as though the assemblyman could hear the thumping of his heart.

'Come on, then, if you have something you want to discuss.'

'Thank you.'

Tsuge followed the man's broad back in. Ukai gestured at the couch but Tsuge set himself down on a chair instead. Ukai took the briefcase from his desk then sank into the couch. He raised his angled features to his visitor. 'Well, what can I do for you?'

'Actually, it's about the upcoming cabinet meeting.' Tsuge made eye contact, his gaze faltering slightly. 'Someone told me you have a question for the police.'

'That's right.'

Ukai had admitted it without hesitation. He looked annoyed, but that was the man's default expression.

'Could I enquire as to the subject? It would help us to—'

'Sorry, not this time.'

Tsuge stiffened at the unexpected force of the man's tone.

'It would only cause you trouble.'

'Why?'

'Because there's no comeback from this one. Look, the best I can do is suggest you get your captain to brush up on begging for forgiveness.'

Tsuge felt himself shiver. It was clear now – Ukai *was* looking for revenge.

'Now, if you'll excuse me.' Ukai took his briefcase and went out into the corridor. He pushed the button on the lift across from his study. The doors slid open.

Tsuge rushed in after him, barely making it.

'Assemblyman. I need to at least know the subject.'

'Oh, you intend to use the lift?'

Members only. Tsuge was only too aware of the rules.

'Get out.'

'. . .'

'What, you think your job entitles you to this?'

'Assemblyman. I just—'

'Leave. Now.'

The doors began to close as Ukai pushed Tsuge out. He watched as the assemblyman – briefcase and all – descended gradually out of sight.

3

It was clear from the tension in the room that the captain was
back. Secretariat Chief Shoichi Sakaniwa was in the visitors' room
to the right. One of the small room's primary functions was to
shield the captain, at least temporarily, from unwanted guests.
The cups of tea on the table inside told Tsuge that Sakaniwa had
just finished dealing with one such guest.

'Can we talk?'

Sakaniwa glanced up from his notebook when Tsuge called
from the door. His expression stiffened when he saw the look on
Tsuge's face. 'What is it?'

'We might have an issue, sir.' Tsuge closed the door behind him
and took a seat. He gave Sakaniwa a brief summary of events.

'A time bomb? What kind of time bomb?'

'I don't know.'

'Can we change his mind?'

'That might be difficult. He seems quite determined.'

Sakaniwa folded his arms and looked up at the ceiling. 'We
need to know what he's going to ask.'

'It could be some kind of dirt, sir. Maybe to do with the
executive.'

Sakaniwa gave Tsuge a wide-eyed stare before looking away.
Dirt. It was a catch-all word for the hidden misbehaviours of the

force. There was some on Sakaniwa, too. Seven years ago, he'd drunk too much and laid into a taxi driver. The driver had been a high-school classmate of Tsuge's, and Tsuge had stepped in on Sakaniwa's request and convinced the man to settle the matter privately. Internal Affairs never heard of the incident, and Sakaniwa had maintained his position in the race to the top.

That spring, Sakaniwa had cleared his debt by bringing Tsuge into the fold. While such transfers were usually the domain of Administration, the man's proximity to the captain afforded him certain privileges and allowed him to essentially handpick his staff.

Tsuge had welcomed the move. He'd been a dyed-in-the-wool member of Security, having spent his whole career in the department, but the Secretariat was special, the domain of the captain, and his sense of ambition had been tickled by the chance to work with the assembly. It would serve him well to become expert in its matters, to gain the confidence of its members, especially in the context of a force that was weak in its external relations. Sakaniwa had himself spent years working with the assembly. One of the main reasons he'd made it to chief of the Secretariat, despite his obvious lack of social nous, was because the captain, together with the bureaucrats in Tokyo, needed someone who could maintain the relationship between the assembly and the force.

Still, it was a double-edged sword to work with the assembly. While success guaranteed a bright career, failure was certain to end one.

'If Ukai won't tell us. . .' Sakaniwa seemed to consider something for a moment. He looked Tsuge in the eye. 'I seem to remember you have a contact in Internal Affairs?'

'Yes.'

Inspector Shindo. The man had effectively been a go-between for Tsuge's marriage, having introduced him to the daughter of a distant relation when they'd both been in Security.

'I want you to see if he knows anything about this. If he's hesitant to commit, tell him this is the direct concern of the captain.'

'Understood.'

'And try the assembly again, see if you can't get some more details.' There was a sudden buzzing sound. Sakaniwa jumped from the couch. *The captain.* 'Make sure you stay on top of this,' he muttered, fiddling with his tie as he rushed out.

Tsuge walked to the corner of the room and picked up the phone. He called Shindo and asked to meet on the roof. The usual play would be to visit his home at night but speed was of the essence.

Shindo had not yet got there when Tsuge arrived. He sat himself down next to the concrete viewing pillar. The cylindrical object was two metres wide and marked with the name of every city and town in the prefecture and the direction in which they lay. It was modelled after the original in the Metropolitan Police Academy, which pointed at the prefectures. *When it gets hard. When you don't know where to go. You come here and you think of home.* Tsuge had been here just once, eight years ago, but he hadn't looked towards home. He'd glared, instead, in the direction of Tokyo. He could still picture the vast blue sky he'd seen that day.

'Hey.'

Shindo walked into view. He stopped and lit a cigarette.

'You're smoking again? That can't be any good for your stomach.'

'Isn't much left to damage.' There was something in his voice that suggested he'd started to let go. It was harder, since the operation on his stomach and his subsequent transfer to Internal

Affairs, to see in this man the high-flying officer from Security. He looked as though he'd grown old suddenly. Maybe he'd given up his aspirations to reach the top. 'Now, tell me what's so important that you had to call me all the way up here.'

Tsuge proceeded to give him a quick summary of events.

'Attack the police?' Shindo repeated, sounding genuinely surprised.

'Can you think of anything he might have been able to dig up?'

'Nothing that's new. Sorry, can't think of a single thing.'

Shindo told him that Internal Affairs had nothing that could be pinned on the executive. If that was true, it was perhaps an organisational issue that Ukai had come across, something that concerned the force itself. It would be too much work to track down something like that. Of course, Tsuge would still have expected word that Ukai was sniffing around to have reached Internal Affairs, even for something like that.

Yet Shindo was adamant that they'd heard nothing.

Tsuge wondered if it wasn't to do with someone in the executive after all. He knew there were other cases like Sakaniwa's. It was possible that Ukai, with his reach as an assemblyman, had managed to unearth something that even Internal Affairs didn't know about. And Ukai's motivation was a factor to consider. The man was looking to exact revenge. He wouldn't draw the line at exposing some past transgression and presenting it as if it were brand new.

At three o'clock, Shindo got to his feet. Looking off to the distance, he started to speak, quietly, as though to himself.

'You could do worse than check in with Administration.'

'Sorry?'

'With the ace. It's possible he'll have something we don't.'

Tsuge watched Shindo's diminished frame get up and leave,

seeing a different side to the man as he did so. *Shinji Futawatari*. *The ace*. As part of Administration, he specialised in personnel. He also held the record for being the youngest officer to make superintendent in Prefecture D, having secured the promotion at forty. Still relatively new to Administrative Affairs, Tsuge had hardly spoken with the man. Yet he couldn't help feeling irked whenever the name came up in conversation. What had he done to be the subject of such universal praise? Sure, he was good at what he did. But his strengths were applicable only *inside* the force. How, Tsuge wondered, would he fare in the outside world? His influence meant nothing in the assembly, in the halls of government. Surely the project to rebuild the headquarters, left now to gather dust for three years, was a case in point.

Tsuge was still sitting next to the pillar.

I'll get it moving.

He would be the one to rally the conservatives; with Misaki at the front, he would be the one to get the stalled plan back on track. The result? He would be the first officer in the prefecture to make superintendent in his thirties, bringing him ever closer to claiming Futawatari's position as 'ace'.

He walked back down the stairs, taking his time as he made his way along the corridor on the first floor of the main building. The door to Administration was open. A slim man with sloped shoulders sat at a desk towards the back. His peaceful, delicate features angled briefly upwards. Tsuge hadn't been ready for the sharpness in the man's eyes.

He'd already disregarded Shindo's advice. The Secretariat would deal with Ukai. Futawatari's piercing stare had done nothing to shake his resolve.

4

It was a little after seven when Tsuge arrived home. His apartment took up one corner of the third floor. Misuzu greeted him when he pushed on the reinforced metal door, looking anxious.

'Darling, there's something—'

Tsuge pushed his way through, telling her to keep it for later. He picked up the cordless handset and shut himself in the room at the end of the hall. He was tired of her complaining. For the last month, it had been ceramics class. It was the latest obsession of the chief of administration's wife. She looked after the local wives' group and insisted the others join her. Misuzu hated it. She was proud of her slim fingers, which meant it was agony for her to use them to mix clay. When he'd suggested she should give it up, she'd just told him she didn't want to be isolated. And when he'd suggested she should put up with it, she'd fallen silent then started to tug at her hair before finally lashing out at the things around her.

She'd been beautiful, full of a passion for life, when he'd first met her. He'd proposed on their second date. He hadn't forgotten, even now, that he'd been obsessed with her. But she'd thinned out in the ten years since their marriage and now all she did was use him as a sounding board to vent her grievances. It was because of this that he'd begun to question the sense of his decision. Had he really wanted her? Or had he simply been excited, ten years ago, by the fact that she was a relative of his high-flying boss? Was there a part of him now that felt betrayed by witnessing the man's decline, realising that the gamble hadn't paid off? *Work will be work. Home will be home.* He remembered having sworn to maintain the distinction but it had all become jumbled over time. The two worlds. The two sets of emotions.

Focus.

Tsuge forced himself back to the present. He opened the directory listing the details of all the members of the assembly and dialled Sakuma's number.

'Sorry to call so late.'

'Tsuge, right . . .' The assemblyman's tone was apologetic from the start. 'Sorry. I failed to get anything from Ukai. He told me it was none of my business.'

'I see. Thank you for trying.'

'No problem. Doesn't look good, though, does it? It does seem as if he's sitting on something big.'

Tsuge smoked a few cigarettes after the call. He'd vowed never to smoke at work, whatever his stress levels. The captain had given it up, so everyone – starting with Sakaniwa and the director of Administrative Affairs – had opted to follow suit.

He started to call the other assembly members. The conservatives had nothing. Taking a deep breath, he called an assemblyman in the opposition he trusted. Still no leads.

He looked into the living room, still edgy, and saw that Misuzu was in the middle of getting dinner ready. She turned his way.

'Darling, just listen.'

'Uh-huh.'

He thought he'd been clear that he had no intention of hearing her out. Apparently ignoring this, she came over to whisper in his ear.

'It's Morio. He's being bullied at school.'

'What?'

'They steal his satchel, leave him out of things.'

Tsuge felt a sudden chill. He stared into his son's room. He saw the boy, turned away and with his back slouched, his small hands fiddling with the pieces of a board game.

'Morio!'

He'd called out before he had time to think. His eight-year-old son's pudding-bowl haircut rotated. The boy looked beaten down, anxious. He was perhaps expecting his dad to be cross. Tsuge didn't know what to say. He remembered the small town. The tiny world. For a total of nine years in primary and secondary school, Tsuge had been controlled by a boy with snake-eyes. He didn't doubt that he'd looked anxious, too, just like his son did now.

Crush anyone who dares get in your way.

He said nothing. Try as he might, he couldn't think of anything suitable to say to the weak-looking reflection of himself.

5

Mornings were busy in the Secretariat. It was during this time of day that the various division chiefs crowded in with documents requiring the captain's approval.

Among them was Yoshikawa from Transport Guidance, who was acting a little jittery. Brash enough in his own division, he found himself, like many others, a little overawed when he came here. He handed the response to the question on the hit-and-run to Tsuge and left without so much as a word. Tsuge reviewed the content then passed it on to Sakaniwa to give to the captain.

Taking up the question he'd drafted the previous day for Misaki, Tsuge left the office.

Only five days remained until the cabinet meeting. He would head straight for the assembly. Once there, he would see if Misaki had anything more on Ukai. Misaki had tipped him off about the 'bomb'. He must have got the information from someone else first.

Tsuge entered the man's study to find him lounging on the couch, just as before, giving the impression that he hadn't moved.

'Tsuge, you're early.'

He seemed to be in high spirits. When Tsuge handed him the question sheet he stuffed it into his briefcase without so much as a second glance, winking to show he trusted Tsuge's work.

'Assemblyman. The information you gave me, about Ukai—'

'Ah yes. Did you get to the bottom of that?'

'I was actually wondering if you had anything else that might help us.'

'Sorry, I've already told you all I know.'

'Who told you about it?'

'Why, the man himself. He volunteered the information. Told me he was sitting on a time bomb, that it was for the police.'

Something didn't quite fit. It was true that the New Liberal Democratic Club and the New Wave Party shared a common heritage, that they were separated only by the men who stood as their representatives, but why would Ukai go out of his way to share information with a veteran from another faction? He would have known it would stir up a fuss. Unless, of course, that had been his intention. Perhaps Ukai had disseminated the information with the *express purpose* of rocking the boat.

But to what end?

To let us know he has something.

Advance notice, then, of his intention to strike. Maybe he wanted to stand and watch as the force panicked. To get as much gratification as he could from his revenge.

There was, of course, another possibility. *Negotiations.* Ukai was out for something in return and was using the threat as leverage. In this scenario, the advance notice would be a signal for the police to open discussions. Yet Ukai had done nothing to suggest this when Tsuge had seen him the day before. If anything, he'd seemed hell-bent on going ahead with whatever it was he was planning. It could have been nothing more than posturing. Perhaps his intention was to drag things out until the last minute, opening himself to negotiations only once the force had admitted defeat.

'You could pay his people a visit,' Misaki suggested from his place on the couch.

'His people?'

'I'd put money on the chairman of his committee knowing something. Even if he doesn't, you could use him to apply a little pressure. I doubt even Ukai would do anything that went against the wishes of his committee.'

It was a good idea. Rather than Tsuge being thanked for writing the question, it was he who ended up bowing in gratitude as he left the room.

Having returned to the Secretariat to bring Sakaniwa up to speed, Tsuge left the headquarters. It was thirty minutes by car to City K and Ukai's electoral district. He could still hear Sakaniwa's words while he was on his way out: *Make sure this goes away.* The previous night, Sakaniwa had taken it upon himself to reach out to a few of his contacts in the assembly. He'd no doubt been confident in his ability to get an answer but he'd come away empty-handed. His expression had made it clear he'd reconsidered the severity of the threat.

Tsuge crossed the city limits.

He checked his map at each set of lights then pulled up to a parking area when he reached what he guessed to be the right area. He walked into a shop on the main road selling rice and the owner confirmed that Haruo Toyama did, indeed, live in the second building around the corner. It wasn't long, following the man's instructions, before a sign came into view bearing the words: *Electoral Committee for Ichiro Ukai.*

Toyama seemed to be returning from walking his dog. The man was plump, probably the same age as Ukai.

'You're with the police?'

Toyama frowned when he saw Tsuge's card. It was perfectly

understandable. He'd avoided arrest during the election four years ago, but he would have spent hours sweating under the harsh lights of the interrogation rooms. He continued to look uncertain as he invited Tsuge into the traditionally built house.

Deciding there was no need for pleasantries, Tsuge got straight to the point. 'Assemblyman Ukai has informed us that he intends to ask a question relating to the police during the upcoming question-and-answer session. Do you know about this?'

'A question relating to the police?'

'Apparently, he has an issue to take up with us.'

'No. I can't say that I . . .' The man's surprise appeared genuine. He leaned in to ask a question of his own. 'What kind of issue?'

'We don't know. That's why I'm here.'

Toyama was starting to look worried. He requested that Tsuge wait for a moment then began to call the remaining committee leaders. Questions of Ukai aside, it was clear that this man at least had no wish to repeat his history with the force. After hanging up the final call Toyama turned back round.

'Nobody knows a thing about it.'

'Then could you kindly check with Ukai himself?'

'Absolutely. I'll try to catch him this evening.'

Call me once you know. Tsuge left after issuing the request. It felt as though he'd acquired the upper hand. It was clear that Toyama was afraid of the police. That was reassuring. The committee would seek to stop Ukai from using whatever it was he had on the police. He was sure of it. Members of the assembly were nothing without their electorate. Ukai would not go against the will of his committee.

Tsuge relaxed during the drive back, stopping to have lunch at a family-run restaurant. It was almost two when he got back to the Secretariat. Aiko Toda jumped to her feet the moment he entered the room. Ukai, she said, was in the visitors' room.

What?

Toyama must have been too worked up to wait until evening. And the fact that Ukai was here, in the Secretariat, meant it was likely that the committee's attempt to reel him in had not gone according to plan. It was an unwelcome thought. Tsuge suddenly felt nauseous.

He opened the door, forgetting even to knock. He saw Sakaniwa and Ukai, both facing him. He watched as the anger spread across the latter's features.

'You . . . you have the *gall* to threaten a member of my committee . . .'

'Assemblyman, I can assure you that I would never do such a thing. But I have to ask you again. Without us knowing what you intend to ask—'

'Silence!'

Sakaniwa snapped upright on the couch.

'If you do *anything* like this again, I will lodge an immediate and official complaint with the governor. Do you understand?'

'Of course . . .' Sakaniwa yelped an apology, having come to stand next to Tsuge and bowing low enough to expose the back of his neck.

Tsuge followed suit. Lodging a complaint with the governor. It was the single greatest threat Ukai could make.

The assemblyman got to his feet, visibly furious. 'I will tell you now so there is no room for doubt. I have absolutely no intention of reconsidering my plans.'

Tsuge and Sakaniwa's heads stayed down until the door was shut.

'This is getting out of control,' Sakaniwa said, biting his lip.

For a moment, the uninteresting contours of the man's face made him appear weak and unambitious. But Tsuge knew that

Sakaniwa was a driven man. Tsuge was the same, and that was what allowed him to see through the man's exterior, to the anger writhing underneath.

Sakaniwa had been Secretariat chief for three years. He would be up for transfer in the spring. As such, he would be looking for ways to rise above the crowd, to get ahead in the race to the top. His was a post that encouraged people to dream. Should the captain choose, he could reward your talents with a special promotion. Talent wasn't even a precondition. In the past, the captain had ordered promotions that would have stunned anyone in the force, simply because he'd liked the people in question. Ukai's question had come at a key moment in the process. It was only to be expected that Sakaniwa would lose his cool.

'The question. If we at least know the question, we may be able to come up with something to stop him.'

'Agreed.'

Although he'd nodded, Tsuge couldn't think of a single option. Having seen the assemblyman's rage, it was clear he wouldn't negotiate. He was out for revenge and his resolve was unwavering. Seeing him again would not convince him otherwise. And Tsuge had already questioned the rest of the assembly members. The electoral committee, too, had proved useless. Even threats had had no effect.

Unless . . .

Perhaps it was just that the threats hadn't been potent enough. Maybe what they needed was to find something they could pin on Ukai. A weakness. If they could somehow pull the relationship back on to even terms, Ukai would have no choice but to step down.

'Do you know anything we could use against him? We need to threaten him, sir, if we're going to stop this.'

Sakaniwa looked at him, clearly taken aback. 'Nothing comes to mind, but I guess I can take a look.'

It was obvious that he was hesitating. *Threaten a member of the assembly?* The look in his eyes, the lines on his forehead – everything conveyed his uncertainty.

He had the ambition but perhaps he lacked the nerve. Tsuge fought an urge to slap him across the face. *You'd better fix that if you're serious about getting to the top.* He had no intention of letting Sakaniwa drag him down. Returning to his desk, he wasted no time in punching the number of Second Division.

6

The jazz was a painful din. Night. Tsuge was waiting for his colleague Yoshiyuki Mayuzumi in an old café behind the train station. He'd chosen it not for the music but because he knew the noise would drown out their conversation. The wait was long, perhaps mirroring the distance that had grown between them. *I'll be there if I can.* That was what Mayuzumi had said. He was a good man, so the words had lacked bite, but they'd also been devoid of intimacy.

There had been discussions, eight years ago, of Tsuge joining the NPA. He'd been flagged as a potential candidate for the hybrid track, where assistant inspectors who had outperformed their colleagues in the prefectures were brought in to work alongside the regular career officers in Tokyo. Tsuge had been torn. Should he take up the offer? Should he go to Tokyo? The decision was like having to choose between staying as an ace pitcher in the minor league and transferring to become an usher in the major. Standing next to the concrete viewing pillar, he'd decided, in the end, to stay. To become the ace. He hadn't attended a social gathering with his contemporaries since. Having turned down his shot at the fast track, he couldn't stomach the idea of any of them getting ahead of him. And his focus had paid off – he ranked above them all. He was competing now with officers who had joined the force three or even four years before him.

The door opened just as he ordered his second coffee.

'Here!' Tsuge called out, raising a hand. He tried not to cringe at the bounce in Mayuzumi's step as he came over.

'Tsuge, it's been a long time.'

Tsuge grimaced. The man was too honest. He hadn't meant it as a jibe, of course, but it clearly wasn't the way to greet someone who worked in the same building as you every day. Mayuzumi had been in Second Division for a good number of years. His gentle manner belied a man who specialised in the investigation of white-collar crime, including corruption, extortion and election fraud.

Ignoring Mayuzumi's attempts to reminisce about old times, Tsuge cut straight to the chase. 'You were part of the investigation into Ukai's election committee.'

'Sure. Good days.'

'Has Ukai been involved in anything untoward?'

Mayuzumi chuckled. 'Of course. That's how we built the case.'

'Not that. Has he been involved in anything since?'

'Tsuge,' Mayuzumi said, then sighed before he continued. 'You've got to be honest with me if you're going to ask questions like that. Why would you want something on Ukai?'

'Because . . .'

Tsuge stopped himself there. Over and above any concerns regarding confidentiality, the real issue was that he didn't want Mayuzumi to see he was in need of help. The noise seemed to move up a notch, insinuating itself into the gap in conversation.

'You know, there's something I've come to understand,' Mayuzumi began, as though to himself. 'You can't make new friends after thirty. You'll have colleagues you work closely with, sure, maybe even a few you'll trust. But they won't be friends, not really. You've got to know each other's flaws, the messed-up shit. Last chance for that's in your twenties, when you're still rough around the edges. Doesn't count after that.'

It dawned on Tsuge that this was the reason Mayuzumi had agreed to meet. Back in police school, he'd struggled to learn how to take down an opponent. He'd failed again and again, regardless of how many times he tried. Mayuzumi had shown him how to read the attack. Only then had Tsuge claimed his first success. Unarmed, he'd knocked a man with a dagger to the ground. Mayuzumi had worn a huge grin when Tsuge had, without thinking, reached out to shake him by the hand.

Tsuge got to his feet.

'I'm sorry you had to come all this way.'

'Tsuge, listen—'

'I want something on Ukai. That's all.'

'Fine. Just sit down.' Mayuzumi reached for a nearby pile of napkins. He took one and began to scribble something down. A name. An address. 'Talk to him. Maybe he'll be able to help.'

'Thanks, I owe you one.'

'Sure, whatever.'

Mayuzumi looked up, his eyes full of pity. From Tsuge's perspective, the eyes belonged to a man already two ranks his junior, one who'd be fetching balls until the day he hung up his uniform. Tsuge took the napkin and the bill and turned around. He needed to get away from the jazz, and from the man's eyes, which were now trained on his back.

Tatsuhiko Seshima. Tsuge recognised the name; it belonged to a detective who had worked in Theft.

He was fifty. A kind, sociable man, these traits had eventually brought him down when he'd ended up sleeping with the wife of a man he'd sent to prison for larceny. He'd been expelled from the force as a result. Thirteen years had passed since. He'd jumped from one job to another before finally landing himself a role as 'strategist' in Ukai's electoral committee. Many of the political parties were firm believers in the benefits of having someone from the force on the payroll. They saw it as a kind of insurance. Yet the last election had shown just how little protection this afforded. Seshima had lost his job and currently worked as a salesman for an import-car dealer.

Having learned this much about the man's background, Tsuge left to pay the man a visit in City I. They'd already spoken on the phone. When he'd told Seshima he wanted to talk about Ukai, the man had invited him to make the trip over.

His home was nicer than expected. A handsome woman in her forties, perhaps the larcenist's wife, came in gracefully with a tray of tea. Tsuge realised he was nervous as he sat on the couch, knowing he needed to be cautious. Seshima might have been police, once, but he was a civilian now. There was no telling where the information might end up if he let it slip that he was out for something to pin on Ukai.

'I warned them not to, you know. But Toyama was panicking, kept saying we'd lose the election unless we did something. That's when they started throwing money around.' Assuming Tsuge was there to discuss the events of the past, Seshima began to give him the lowdown.

'Ukai knew about the bribes, of course.'

'Ukai? Not at all. He was kept in the dark about the whole thing.'

The defensive tone came as a surprise. Seshima had been fired from his role in the committee so Tsuge had naturally assumed he'd hold a grudge. That didn't seem to be the case.

'He might not look it, you know, but the man's a coward. He was shaking when Second Division came through the door. I was, too, mind.' Seshima's lips approximated a smile, but it fell short of reaching his eyes.

'I'll bet he really hates the force.'

'Ukai? I don't think so. Now, I can't comment on what goes on inside that head of his, but I've never heard him criticise the police. Not once.'

'Hmm.'

There was silence as Tsuge considered this. Seshima muttered something, a name.

'Who?'

'Junichi Yamane. I don't suppose you know what he's busy with these days? I heard he'd switched to First Division.'

Of course. Seshima would want to catch up on news regarding his old colleagues in Criminal Investigations. Tsuge decided he would humour him for a while. He didn't know much about current investigations, nor did he recognise the majority of names the man gave him, but he managed nonetheless to satisfy his curiosity with a few inconsequential snippets of information. Tsuge felt himself relax. At least a part of Seshima still considered himself to be an officer of the law.

'There's something else I'd like to ask, if you don't mind?'

'Sure.'

'Do you know of anything that might compromise Ukai's position?'

'Compromise his position?' Seshima looked up.

'I need to find something I can pin on him. It's a matter of urgency.'

'Why? What happened?'

'He's planning to take revenge, for the election.'

'No way. He's too much of a coward to do something like that.'

'He's already made his intentions very clear.'

With this, Seshima's certainty seemed to waver. He seemed to weigh something up before he opened his mouth to speak again.

'There is, I suppose, a woman . . .'

Tsuge's mind worked hard during the drive back. *Kinue Taiyo. Works at a nightclub.* Ukai had been involved with the woman for three years, and this despite the fact that his wife had passed away only a year ago. Still, it didn't seem like it was enough. It could still be rationalised as a relationship between two consenting adults. The one sticking point, perhaps, was the fact that the woman was a worker at a nightclub. Even then, it seemed to fall short as a countermeasure, regardless of how he tried to present it.

There was something else that had caught his attention – Seshima's assessment of Ukai's personality. Tsuge's impression, after half a year of working with the man, was of someone who was difficult but practical. Yet he'd come across as headstrong and obstinate since declaring his intention to attack. And Seshima had described the man as a coward. None of the descriptions seemed to match. It was as though Ukai were in possession of three separate personalities. There was no doubt that he had suffered at the hands of the police. Yet Seshima had argued that the man lacked nerve, that he would never position himself against the Prefectural HQ. The latter, at least, seemed to tally with Tsuge's own impression. Not once had he seen in Ukai anything to suggest that the man harboured a grudge. And yet he *had* declared his intention to attack. And now, some four years on from the election.

Tsuge lit a cigarette.

He crushed two, then three, stubs in the car's built-in ashtray. The cabinet meeting was only three days away. Time was growing short, and he'd learned nothing of Ukai's true intentions, or about the nature of the explosive in his possession. *The question. The captain being forced to apologise.* The numbers on the digital clock seemed, in that moment, like those on the timer of a bomb.

8

Tsuge was just as anxious and frustrated when September's cabinet meeting was called into session. The question-and-answer
session had, fortunately, been scheduled for the second day of
the proceedings. That would be when Ukai would take to the
podium.

For the last three days Tsuge had made a daily pilgrimage to
the assemblyman's home in City K. He'd learned nothing new,
except the name and voice of Ukai's housekeeper. He didn't even
know if Ukai had genuinely been out or had just been pretending
to be.

'Have you told the captain?'

'Not yet.'

Not for the first time that day, Tsuge and Sakaniwa had gathered in the visitors' room to discuss the matter in private. There
was no longer any choice but to accept that Ukai could not
be appeased. Their next step was clear: find out the nature of
the question. If they did that, they could at least try to draft a
response, however devastating the revelation turned out to be. It
would be awkward, nothing more than a stop-gap measure, but
it would at least give the impression that the captain had made a
considered response. They could not allow him to be blindsided,
leave him to panic with nothing to say.

The reputation of the headquarters would be in tatters.

In addition to his gnawing anxiety, Tsuge found himself inundated with desk work. The captain had returned the draft responses, together with plenty of red marker pen. He'd devoted what seemed a significant amount of time to purging them of any words or phrases that came across as overly bureaucratic. That was fine, but the upcoming session was not the usual guarded affair. In it lurked a terrorist who hoped to destabilise the very foundation on which the Prefectural HQ stood.

Tsuge and Sakaniwa reconvened that evening.

'Here, perhaps you can use this.' Sakaniwa slid a memo across the table. On it, written in pen, was an address and room number for an apartment in City D. *Kinue Taiyo. The woman from the nightclub.* Sakaniwa had, it seemed, been busy following up on Tsuge's lead.

'This is where she lives?'

'The room's in Ukai's name, but it seems she stays here. This is the only chance we're going to get. Use her to pressure him into talking.'

Sakaniwa's tone was that of a man backed into a corner. But Tsuge wasn't doing this as a favour – he was in exactly the same position. If Ukai saw this through, they would both end up taking the fall.

'Take this with you.'

Sakaniwa pushed a paper bag into Tsuge's arms. It contained what seemed to be an expensive bottle of spirits.

Nine o'clock. Tsuge stood outside the room on the seventh floor of the apartment complex, paper bag in hand. Knowing Ukai wouldn't let him in if Kinue was there, he'd opted for a time that was busy in her trade. An empty bracket hung above the door, the kind that usually housed a security camera. His fingers were trembling slightly when he pushed the buzzer. After a short wait the door opened to reveal Ukai in a bathrobe.

'You again.'

He looked as annoyed as ever but Tsuge thought he could see alarm in the man's expression. He hadn't committed a crime per se but Tsuge doubted there were many members of the assembly who could remain impassive when caught in a love nest they'd set up for a woman of the night. And yet it would still all be over if Ukai chose to slam the door in his face. Tsuge took a deep breath before he spoke.

'Assemblyman, I just need a moment of your time. I'll make sure I'm gone before she gets here.'

Ukai removed his glasses and glared straight into Tsuge's eyes. 'Are you trying to imply something?'

'Just ten minutes. That's all I need.'

'. . .'

'Assemblyman, please.'

'Make it quick.'

Tsuge gave a deep bow of his head then followed the man into the living room.

'You've got ten minutes, no more. Push it and I call the governor. Are we clear?'

The phone in his hands began to ring the moment he finished speaking, causing him to tut.

'This is Ukai. Uh-huh. Wait, just what the hell do you mean by that?' The assemblyman's eyes darted briefly in Tsuge's direction. He got up from the couch and said, 'Hang on a second, I'm going into the other room.'

It seemed there was something he didn't want overheard. Ukai turned towards Tsuge and told him he was free to leave whenever he wanted. He disappeared into the bedroom and shut the door.

Left alone, Tsuge realised how nervous he'd become. *What was the matter with him? Just get it done.* He glowered at the bedroom door, noticing something on the floor as he did so. Ukai's briefcase. It was right there, beside the couch. His pulse quickened. He looked back at the door, then at the briefcase. He gave the door another wary glance.

He was moving before he even registered that he'd made the decision. Raising himself up a little from the couch, he began to shuffle sideways. He leaned forwards to listen in to the bedroom. Ukai was talking. Completely absorbed, it seemed, in whatever it was he was discussing. Tsuge sat back down. Once at the edge of the couch, he dropped one knee to the ground. Keeping his eyes on the door, he reached out for the briefcase. His fingers registered the cool touch of the surface. Quietly, he undid the clasp.

There were documents inside. His heart was pounding so hard it was a struggle even to breathe. He grabbed at the papers with sweaty fingers. He flicked through them one by one. A paper on environmental hormones. Statistics on small and medium businesses filing for bankruptcy. A pamphlet advertising life insurance. Another paper. A handwritten memo. A list of names from his committee. More statistics. Another list of names, this one for some kind of reunion. More papers. More papers. Still more papers. There was nothing inside to even hint at what the man's question might be. Nothing that had anything to do with the police.

Damn it.

There was a noise from the bedroom. Tsuge fell back on to the couch. In the next moment, Ukai opened the door and came back in. He seemed to cotton on to the fact that something was wrong.

'Are you okay?'

'I'm fine . . .' Tsuge realised his back was soaked with sweat.

'That's your ten minutes up. Time to leave.'

'I can't leave, not until I know what you intend to ask,' Tsuge said, his guilty conscience lending new force to his words. Perhaps it was the desperation. He'd seen nothing of the 'time bomb' in Ukai's briefcase, which probably meant the details of the question existed only in the head of the man standing before him. 'I need to know. Just a few words will do.'

'You'll find out tomorrow.'

'That's too late. It's vital that I know today.'

'Your problem, not mine.'

Tsuge's teeth cut into his lip. This would be what people called bloodlust. He felt a powerful urge to beat the man senseless, to drag him off the couch and give him a good kicking. But it was Tsuge who got to his feet. He crumpled on to his knees. His hands hit the ground. He told himself it was just an act, even as he shook with rage and humiliation.

'I'll be in your debt. I'm begging you, please.'

He brought his head even closer to the carpet. His cheeks were on fire. Blood coursed through his temples. The few centimetres left between his forehead and the floor were all that remained of his pride. He let go of that, too. He thought he would choke on the synthetic smell of the fibres. His heart was already elsewhere. He saw Morio and the boy with the snake-eyes. He ran from them, too. He wanted the clear blue sky. The sky he'd seen that day at the viewing pillar, back when he'd still burned with raw ambition.

'If you're this good at kowtowing, you might want to consider running for election.'

Tsuge's head snapped up, only to see Ukai holding out the bag with the alcohol in it. The assemblyman flashed a grin.

'I'll see you in the hall tomorrow.'

9

The assembly hall, decorated in lavish marble and expensive wood, was bathed in a warm and dignified glow. Tsuge was in the waiting room behind it, unable to move from his seat. The question-and-answer session was already underway. Misaki's voice was stately as it carried through the tannoy system on the wall.

. . . the unforgivable cowardice of the driver has sparked outrage in our community and caused a great deal of sadness and fear. We must not allow this to go . . .

Tsuge paid the man little attention. The room bustled around him as civil servants with stacks of documents hurried this way and that. They were standing by, having prepared a variety of documents to field any unexpected questions. Tsuge had nothing.

Assemblyman Ichiro Ukai, if you would be so kind as to take to the podium.

The tannoy shook with the deep register of the chairman's voice. Tsuge held his breath. Time was up. Ukai was going to detonate the bomb.

The assemblyman's voice began to fill the room.

The risks posed by environmental hormones, currently the subject of much attention in the papers and on television, are now too great to be . . .

Following the order of business, Ukai opened with a question on environmental hormones then moved on to another regarding policy and small and medium businesses. That was now drawing to a close.

Ukai coughed once, clearing his throat. For a moment there was silence. Tsuge closed his eyes. His hands clawed into his knees. His chest seemed to constrict. Ukai was speaking again. Sucked into the vacuum of Tsuge's mind, the words took a while to form.

I thank you in advance for your considered response. That is all.
What?

Tsuge stared at the speaker on the wall. Was that it? Ukai had finished?

We do, of course, consider the issue of environmental hormones to be one of the utmost importance. As such, we have put in motion plans to . . .

The chief of Environment and Sanitation began to read out his response. Tsuge broke into a run. He inched open the door that led to the hall and scanned the area usually reserved for members of the assembly. Ukai was back in his seat, wearing his trademark look of annoyance. Leaning a little to the side, he was nodding as he listened to the chief's answer.

Ukai had finished. He really had finished.

Tsuge's feet dragged as he returned via the underground passage. He felt a mixture of relief and exhaustion, even as his mind busied itself with questions.

Why?

Why hadn't the assemblyman followed through with his threat? Had he buckled under pressure from his committee? Had it been something to do with the call he'd taken the previous evening?

Or . . .

Tsuge was struck by a thought. What if he'd never had anything to start with? What if Ukai had only *claimed* to have something? Was that it? If so, for what reason? Maybe he'd wanted the police to panic. That didn't make sense, though – his actions hadn't had any impact on the force as a whole. They'd concerned only the Secretariat. Thinking about it, Tsuge realised that only Sakaniwa and himself had been affected. They were the only two who had suffered. Had that been Ukai's intention? Again, the question remained: Why?

Who the fuck knows.

The door to the visitors' room was open when he got back to the Secretariat. He saw the chiselled features of a private-sector CEO, one who had been there on a few previous occasions. Sakaniwa was there, too, sitting with his back to the door as he listened to what the man had to say.

Tsuge took a seat at his desk. For a moment, everything seemed to go dark. His eyes traced slowly back to the other room, fearful, as though he'd seen a ghost.

Sakaniwa. His back to the door.

That was normal enough. The couches were arranged so that Sakaniwa could – and always did – offer the furthest one to visitors while he sat with his back to the door. *But not that time.* Tsuge had returned to the office following his meeting with Toyama. Hearing that Ukai was already in attendance, he'd opened the door to the room without so much as knocking. He'd seen Ukai and Sakaniwa's faces together. Ukai had looked annoyed but that was the man's default expression. He hadn't been angry, then, not until Tsuge had shown up. Not while he'd been sitting beside the chief.

Had they been in collusion? Tsuge considered the idea. There was, he had to admit, one thing that lent traction to the theory. Not once had Sakaniwa tried to dissuade Ukai in person. He'd delegated all the work to Tsuge. Sakaniwa was himself a veteran when it came to working with the assembly. It went without saying that he and Ukai would know each other. Despite this, and regardless of the fact that his own head was on the line, he hadn't gone to see the man in person. Did that mean they'd been working together? That it had been some form of entrapment? No, it couldn't be anything like that. He'd been made to do the legwork, that was all. No harm had come of it. Besides, he didn't believe either of them had reason to hold a grudge against him.

I'm getting paranoid.

'Tsuge.' Sakaniwa came over, having already emerged from the visitors' room. 'I guess we should call this a win.'

'Sir, I suppose. But—'

'By the way,' Sakaniwa went on, lowering his voice, 'someone told me Ukai filed a theft report with district.'

'A theft report?'

'Yes. It seems that someone saw fit to steal the man's briefcase,' he said, a faint smile playing across his lips.

Tsuge watched, mouth gaping, as the chief walked away. *Briefcase. Theft.* For a while everything seemed lost in a haze. Tsuge failed to notice Aiko Toda offer him coffee. *Briefcase.* He started to shake. *Briefcase. Prints. Camera. Trap.* The words came together to form a cohesive but unexpected narrative. The story belonged neither to him nor to Assemblyman Ukai. Instead, it belonged to Secretariat Chief Shoichi Sakaniwa.

The man was hoping for a significant promotion come the next round of transfers. He would do all he could to secure himself a post as director. Before that, however, he had to first rid himself of the one blemish that could come back to haunt him.

His one mistake, made seven years ago.

The plan had already been in motion when he'd called Tsuge to join the Secretariat. He'd spun out the idea of the 'time bomb' and made damn sure that Tsuge felt the pressure. He'd understood that Tsuge's instinct for self-protection would compel him to lay hands on the briefcase. There hadn't been a doubt in his mind.

It was Sakaniwa who had called Ukai at his apartment the previous evening. He'd wanted to ensure that Tsuge was left alone with the briefcase. There'd been the empty bracket above the main door, the kind that housed a security camera. The camera itself would have been hidden, he guessed, in the room with him. Ukai would have kept watch from the bedroom, prolonging the call until Tsuge had done the deed.

The briefcase had not been stolen. If Tsuge should ever come to pose a threat, it would turn up at a substation in some town. It would be flagged as the stolen property of one of the prefecture's key assembly members. As such, it would be sent for forensics testing. Tsuge's prints would be found plastered over all the papers inside.

The officer who stole an assemblyman's briefcase.

The fact would never become public knowledge but it would mark the end of his career in the force.

Still, that wasn't how the story had panned out. Tsuge would, of course, never breathe a word about Sakaniwa's past transgression. *Keep things on an even keel.* The story was over the moment Sakaniwa got what he needed.

Ukai had played a role, albeit a bit part, in the story. As Seshima had seen, the man was a coward at heart. The investigation had been devastating, and he'd been at the mercy of the force ever since. When Sakaniwa, one of the closest aides to the captain, had approached him for a favour, he'd jumped at the chance to earn some goodwill.

Yet Tsuge couldn't help wondering whether there hadn't been something more to the man's ready agreement to become an accomplice. He recalled the ferocity of the anger Ukai had directed his way. Perhaps the man had decided to use him as a punchbag, as a means of venting his pent-up animosity.

This would, of course, never be more than conjecture. These were questions no one would answer.

He glanced at Sakaniwa's desk. In profile, the chief's unremarkable features had even less impact. Tsuge was surprised to find that he bore the man no ill will. He suspected he'd have done something similar in Sakaniwa's position.

It'll come in useful, some day.

He had to admit, the thought had been there at the back of his mind.

The Secretariat returned to its usual quiet that afternoon.

Tsuge saw the brown roof of the archives beyond the window. A narrow strip of blue sky peeked out from above.

10

The apartment was dark when Tsuge arrived home.

Misuzu and Morio were in the next town along, at Misuzu's family home. The school had granted them leave as an emergency measure to escape the bullying, which had apparently grown worse.

Tsuge sipped at a bowl of noodles. He turned on the washing machine and started to run a bath but turned the tap off halfway. He collapsed into bed. He lay there for a while, arms and legs spread like a cross. There was a drawing of him on the wall. Scribbled in paint and crayon, he didn't think it much of a likeness. The words were a mess, too.

Thanks for working so hard.

Tsuge put on his clothes and left the building. There was something he needed to tell his son. He held on to the words as he set out in the car:

Make a friend. Just one will do.

He wasn't sure if he really believed them, but he pushed down on the accelerator regardless, as though to stamp out the apathy growing inside him.